Randy Kay has the perfec  adorable son. But Randy' and everyone who knows him. He's gay.

Marriage and fatherhood, which he thought could change him, have failed. He doubts if anyone can love him for who he really is—especially himself.

With his wife's blessing, he sets out to explore the gay world he's hidden from all his life.

John Walsh, a paramedic with the Chicago Fire Department, is comfortable in his own skin as a gay man, yet he can never find someone who shares his desire to create a real relationship, a true family.

When Randy and John first spy each other in Chicago's Boystown, all kinds of alarms go off—some of joy, others of deep-seated fear.

Randy and John must surmount multiple hurdles on the journey to a lasting, meaningful love. Will they succeed or will their chance at love go up in flames, destroyed by missed connections and a lack of self-acceptance?

UNRAVELING

Rick R. Reed

A NineStar Press Publication

Published by NineStar Press
P.O. Box 91792,
Albuquerque, New Mexico, 87199 USA.
www.ninestarpress.com

Unraveling

Printed in the USA
First Edition
January, 2020

Print ISBN: 978-1-951880-17-0

Also available in eBook, ISBN: 978-1-951880-16-3

Warning: This book contains sexually explicit content, which may only be suitable for mature readers.

In memory of John Y. and Curt E.
Both gone too soon.

"...an unraveling—a time when you feel a desperate pull to live the life you want to live, not the one you're 'supposed' to live. The unraveling is a time when you are challenged by the universe to let go of who you think you are supposed to be and to be and to embrace who you are."

—Brene Brown

"The most terrifying thing is to accept oneself completely."

—C.G. Jung

"I'm nothing great. But I'm a rose... I'm a rose whether I'm admired or not, I'm a rose whether anyone's crazy about me or not... Like I said, nothing great. Just a rose... But, do you know what it means to be a rose, my friend? Being a rose means 'freedom.' It means not existing by the praises of others or not ceasing to exist by their disapproval."

—Serdar Özkan

1986, Winter

Golden Slumbers

Golden slumbers kiss your eyes,

Smiles awake you when you rise;

Sleep, pretty wantons, do not cry,

And I will sing a lullaby,

Rock them, rock them, lullaby.

Care is heavy, therefore sleep you,

You are care, and care must keep you;

Sleep, pretty wantons, do not cry,

And I will sing a lullaby,

Rock them, rock them, lullaby.

By Thomas Dekker

Chapter One

RANDY

I have my death all planned out.

Unlike the thirty-two years that have gone before, I want my passing to be peaceful and free of the discord and pain I've lived with for as long as I can remember. I want it to be easy. Effortless. Guilt-free.

Whether it's any of those things remains to be seen.

I've rented this hotel room at a small boutique hotel off Michigan Avenue. The Crewe House has been standing on this same ground on Oak Street for at least a hundred years. The rooms are small, fussy, and charming, with flocked wallpaper, four-poster beds, and claw-foot tubs and pedestal sinks in their black-and-white bathrooms. It's charming, and I deserve something nice to gaze at before I close my eyes for good.

I have some sandalwood-scented candles lit, and the fragrance is warm, enveloping. Their soft flicker is the only illumination. Outside, the winter sky darkens early. Dusk's cobalt blue makes silhouettes of the water towers, train tracks, and buildings to the west of the hotel. Near the horizon the sky is a shade of lavender that mesmerizes me, makes me think of changing my mind. If a sky like this can exist, with its electric bands of color, maybe the world isn't such a horrible place.

Maybe I can go on.

No.

What else have I done to ease my passage into whatever comes next? I have a bottle of Veuve Cliquot, my favorite champagne, uncorked and resting in a silver ice bucket, filled with melting ice. A flute stands next to it, waiting.

I'll wash the sleeping pills down with the bubbly.

Before getting into bed, I'll turn on the cassette I have in my boombox, *Abbey Road*. I have it queued up to "Golden Slumbers."

I've been carrying this weight for such a long time.

I long for smiles.

At last, I'll undress and stretch out on the four-poster. I'll pull the eiderdown duvet loosely over me and close my eyes.

The plan is I will slowly slip under, my brain becoming a soft velvety fog, and I'll simply fall into the arms of a comforting—and obliterating—slumber.

I will not dream.

It won't take long.

And I'll leave a beautiful corpse.

That's the plan, anyway. Some of my research into this method of offing myself runs counter to this gentle fantasy, but I don't want to consider the downside of overdosing on strong barbiturates.

I want to go to sleep.

I want to forget the impossibility of being able to become the man I know I should be.

Husband.

Father.

I blink back tears as I sit on the bed, staring out at the deepening twilight. *They don't deserve this: what you're going to leave them with.* I know the voice inside, the one that's always made me do the right thing, at the expense of my very being, is right. *And even though they don't deserve it, you know they will hurt, of course they will, but in the end, they'll be better off.*

Who wants a husband and father who can't seem to make himself straight, despite trying therapy, the Catholic Church, the Buddhist faith, self-help groups, and self-help books. A group of pathetic married men meeting once a month and thinking they can change. Nothing works. If I could change, I would.

And since I can't change, I'm left with three options:

Accept myself as I am. How can I do that? I'd be a failure as a husband, a father, a son, a brother. I'd go on wearing this suffocating mask. I'd continue to live a life that's essentially a lie.

Everyone who loves me doesn't even know me.

They love a façade, a projection, a mirage made of wishes, impossible hopes, and self-hatred.

No, acceptance is not an option. It never was.

Second, I could resist. I could knuckle down and brace myself against the attractions I feel, the dreams that pop up in my sleep despite my desperately not wanting them there. I could hold myself back from falling prey to the temptations I feel on the streets, the subway, the locker rooms—everywhere I encounter a beautiful man.

The reason I find myself here is because I can't resist. Not anymore.

And the third option is simply the one I have to choose—remove myself from the pain. Remove myself from existing as this broken thing that God nor man can fix.

Yes, Violet and Henry both will find a way to move on, and they'll be happier, more anchored in life without me.

Who needs a gay dad? Or a husband who, deep down, doesn't want what his wife has to offer? Or worse, a dad who contracts the death sentence of AIDS?

Enough of the grim thoughts. They were not part of my plan. Tonight, I go out peacefully. I'll shut my eyes and remember things like my joy six years ago when Henry was born and seeing him take his first breath. I shouted, "We got a boy!" and fell into the deepest, most effortless love I've ever felt. I'll remember proposing to Violet when we were both college sophomores and the thrill when she accepted the cheap diamond-chips ring I gave her. *Things will be okay now*, I remember thinking. I can change.

I really believed that. And I know I love Violet as best I can.

It's sad when your best simply isn't good enough.

I reach over for the bottle of sleeping pills on the nightstand. There are thirty of them, and I intend to take them all, two or three at a time. If it takes the whole bottle of champagne to get them down, well, things could be worse. No?

I tip the bottle and look at the tablets against the dark wood, so innocent, yet so lethal.

I'm just reaching for one when there's a sudden knock on the door. Loud. Forceful. Urgent.

"Randy? Randy? Open up, please."

The door knob turns as Violet's voice penetrates the heavy wood of the door, making her sound muffled.

I close my eyes. I could ignore her, hope she goes away.

How did she find out where I was anyway?

She wasn't supposed to know until she got the letter, the one neatly folded and an arm's length away on the nightstand.

Pounding. "Please!" Violet calls.

I gather the pills, shoving them back in the bottle, then hide the container in a nightstand drawer.

How will I explain?

I get up, cross the room, and open the door.

Chapter Two

JOHN

My friend Vince listens in sympathetic silence as I clue him in to the details of my latest breakup. In the past year, this latest one marks the fifth time I've been dumped. Hey, if being knocked down a peg or two is good for the old self-esteem, then I should be in great shape, mental-health-wise, right? A real shining example of self-love.

Then why do I feel so shitty?

Vince asks, "So what happened this time?"

I smile a little because I know my best friend's secret. He's hoping he sounds concerned as he asks this question, but I can hear the lust for gossip dancing around the edges of his wanting the details.

I sigh. "Ah. Same old story. Like the guy last September?"

Vince groans sympathetically or at least fake sympathetically. "Married dude?"

"No, nah, not exactly. But he was still with this older guy."

"The one he said was just a roommate? That they'd—"

I finish for him. "That they'd broken up a while back, and he was just staying with him until he could find his own place."

"There are tons of places in Chicago. I found my apartment in a day."

"I know that and you know that, so why didn't he?" I picture Christopher in my mind's eye. He was a big hairy guy, balding at twenty-eight, which only made him more masculine and sexier. And Lord, he was a chef too. He was hot *and* he could cook. I'd thought I'd found my Prince Charming, the one who could rock my world, feed my soul, and more importantly, feed my belly.

Ah, but Christopher had someone else's soul, belly, and nether regions he was rocking all along, despite what he told me. Thinking back now, I recall an old phrase my grandmother used to apply to teenagers, "You know how you tell when a kid is lying?" she'd ask someone, maybe my mom. Mom would shake her head even though she already knew the answer. Grandma would then say, "Their lips move."

Yeah, Christopher was far from being a teenager, but when his lips moved, I had to wonder if they were ever forming truthful words.

"Anyhow," I cut the story short with Vince, whom I hate to admit is probably reveling in the details. He's always been pretend happy for me when I meet someone and then pretend sad when it all goes to shit, as it always does.

Vince is in love with me. He thinks I don't know. But I've known since we first met, back in college at Northern Illinois University, down in DeKalb.

"Anyhow, we're in bed, getting ready to do the nasty. I mean, I'm rolling on a rubber, when the intercom sounds. Guess who?"

Vince gasps, "No!"

"Oh yes, honey, the boyfriend is at my front door. Buzzing and buzzing and screaming like a baby for Chris." I shiver a little at the memory.

"What did you do?"

"What do you think? We kind of froze, at first, in a panic." I shrugged. "Then we got dressed. I opened the door for Christopher and told him I hoped it all would go okay."

He'd asked me if I'd see him again. There were tears in his eyes. *Sorry, buddy.*

I simply shook my head as I closed the door behind him.

"Since then, he's been calling. And calling. But I just let the answering machine pick up. His tears don't move me. He begs me to reconsider. He tells me how Patrick, his sugar daddy, threw all his clothes out on their lawn up in Kenilworth. He says he really loves me."

"You gonna give him another chance?" I detect that Vince hopes I'll say no. I give him his wish.

"Hell, no. I don't trust him. And when trust is gone, there's nothing."

Vince breathes out a sigh of relief. "You got that right."

"I'm always right." I laugh. Unfortunately. Like in the way I believe every guy I connect with is gonna be *the one*, until he isn't anymore. I always know. And it makes my stomach turn.

I pray I'm not always right when I think I'm a bird with a damaged wing who will never, ever find love...only gossip with a best bud who hopes I realize he's the perfect man for me.

Sorry, Vince, not by a long shot.

I do a quick mental check before I tell Vince I need to go, and I'll see him this coming Thursday on Halsted for comedy night at the video bar, Sidetracks. We never miss comedy night because even if we don't meet a man, at least we have some laughs.

My mental check reveals that hope is still there, its heart beating a bit fainter, but still hammering away, waiting.

Chapter Three

VIOLET

When Randy finally opens the door, I'm shocked. My heart feels like it's twisting in on itself. I let out a shaky breath. I want to cry, but I grit my teeth and hold back my tears. I know this is not my time.

He needs me.

He doesn't *know* he needs me, and he may not ever need me like a husband needs a wife. But I love him, dammit, and I'm here to save him.

His handsome face, usually a lovely Mediterranean olive tone, is pale and ashy. His dark brown eyes are red, the area around them puffy. He looks like he's heading into the worst flu of his life.

But he's not heading into a physical sickness. He's poised straight for mental anguish; the kind of despair someone feels when they abandon hope. The kind of thing when darkness fades into black.

"Randy?" I manage to whisper. I reach my hand out to touch his dark grizzled cheek, but he moves back like a frightened animal.

"What are you doing here?"

The question is said as a kind of moan, born maybe of frustration, sadness, rage, regret? I don't know. I'm here to find out.

"How did you find me?"

I cock my head at him. "Really, Randy? Is that what matters? How I found you?" I move a step or two into the room, testing. I'm grateful he moves back and opens the door a bit wider.

I move past him into the room. It's dark. The only illumination are rows of flickering candles. It strikes me not as sad or somber, but creepy like something out of a horror movie. My gaze moves to the bed to check for a corpse, all laid out. I stride over to a floor lamp next to an overstuffed leather wing chair. I turn it on to lend some warmer, yellow light to the room.

The curtains are open and the night outside presses in like some dark, living thing. In the glow of a streetlamp just to the right of the window, snow falls in an illuminated cone.

Randy cowers near that window. I want to take him in my arms, but again, common sense and my own instincts tell me now is not the time.

I do, however, manage a smile. "Do we have to stand?"

In response, he sits gingerly on the edge of the bed. He doesn't look at me. Instead he regards his fingernails, which I know he's chewed to the bloody quick.

I take the wing chair. I notice the ice bucket and the bottle of champagne. *Veuve Cliquot*. It's always been Randy's favorite. I lean forward and gesture toward it. "Going to share?"

He looks over at the ice bucket and the bottle, and it's as though, for the briefest of moments, he's wondering how it got there. He gets up from the bed and sighs. Maybe he's disappointed he'll have to share. "Sure."

He pours a glass for me in the single champagne flute set out. He looks around for another one and ends up pouring himself some in one of the plastic cups from the bathroom. He hands me the champagne and then turns to go back to his place on the bed.

We're not going to toast.

He takes a sip and asks me again, "What are you doing here?"

I swallow a bit of the champagne. The bubbles tickle my nose. I drink some more, and finally, I drain the whole glass in a quick swallow. I stand, despite the tremble I feel in my knees, and refill my glass. I blow out a big breath and sit again, pulling at a loose thread on my jeans. I set my glass down and hug myself. "It's cold in here."

Randy simply nods. He's waiting.

I came here for a reason. I know a lot more than he realizes. It's time to start to tell him the truth, what I know, what I've known now for a couple of years, but buried in my own wishful thinking and denial.

I force myself to meet his gaze—those dark brown eyes I fell in love with as a sophomore at Miami University in the charming little college town of Oxford, Ohio. Randy was in the lobby of my dorm with a girl from my floor, Kathy Burt. At first, I despaired, thinking they were a couple. To my relief, I found out quickly they were best friends. There was nothing romantic between them.

That was good because I think I fell in love with Randy in that short moment in the dorm lobby. I think of how I read somewhere love at first sight isn't really first sight at all—it's falling in love all over again with a lover from a past life. When I looked into Randy's eyes, so brown the pupil got lost in the chocolate of his irises, I swear to God I thought this was the guy I was going to marry one day.

We'd made awkward small talk, how the summer was lingering so late into fall. What dorm are you in? Or do you live off campus? What's your major? All the while casting glances at Kathy, whom I didn't know well, trying to telepathically communicate the message that I wanted to arrange a more meaningful meeting with this beautiful, skinny boy with his mop of black hair and eyes that had the power to hypnotize.

Kathy came through and arranged for us to meet up— not a real date, but it turned into one. We shared a pitcher of 3.2 beer at a bar uptown (because back then eighteen-year-olds could drink 3.2) and talked until the lights came up in the little wood-paneled joint with its peanut shells on the floor. Pure Prairie League was singing, "Amy." Dan Fogelberg. Boston. Heart.

Randy walked me back to my dorm and put his arm around me. At the front door, he didn't ask to come in. He didn't even try to kiss me.

So I kissed him, tasting beer on his tongue and wanting, so much, to invite him up to my room. But I wasn't that kind of girl. I could only hope he'd try to persuade me. All these guys I'd warded off at this very door, and the one I wanted to push me a little in a wicked direction doesn't deliver! Begrudgingly, I imagined, I would give in, leading him up the stairs, our fingers entwined.

But Randy simply turned toward the quad after our kiss. I thought, in the light from the front porch lanterns, that his cheeks were a little rosier, glowing. Now I wonder if I was imagining things.

We agreed to meet at King Library the next night after dinner to hang out and study together.

He was an English major, and I was in the business school. I wondered if it could work. But, oh, how I wanted it to!

Back in the present, I fess up. "I followed you here."

He stares, the suspicion in his eyes making them shine, I think, a little brighter. "Why?" he wonders.

I close my eyes for a moment. "I know. Everything."

Of course, I know he'll play dumb. And he does.

"What are you talking about?"

I decide to begin with the most recent revelation. The one that set me on his trail. The one that got me here, in this hotel room, thanking God I'm not too late.

"Walgreens called this morning. The pharmacy. You'd left your credit card on the counter."

Randy's skin pales. And maybe a sickly yellowish sheen is creeping in.

"So?"

"So I went down to get it. And, ethical or legal or not, the pharmacist mentioned the sleeping pills. He knew we were married, and he wanted me to be sure to tell you to be careful with them, especially at first. They're strong. No alcohol." I glance over at the bottle of champagne.

I know my voice breaks a little as I say, "Randy. One thing about you is you never have trouble sleeping. I know because I'm the one with insomnia. I'm the one who's awake in the middle of the night, envying your snores." I laugh, but it comes out fake. Flat.

I'd pieced together the puzzle. He must have picked up the prescription before work. He was an advertising copywriter for a gadgets catalog on Michigan Avenue.

When he called to say he had to stay late at work at around three, I hopped on the L and headed downtown, hoping I'd not be too late to see him emerge from his building. I needed to know where he was going with all those sleeping pills.

Working late, my ass.

Randy nods as he absorbs the knowledge.

I lean forward a little and ask, "Where are they?"

He doesn't try to dodge the question. He points to the nightstand drawer. "In there."

I get up and cross the room to open the drawer. The amber pill bottle is there, next to a bible and a small pad of paper and pen. With a shaking hand, I pick up the bottle and quietly slip it in the pocket of my coat.

He doesn't try to stop me.

I spy the folded piece of paper on the nightstand, and although I yearn to pick it up and read it, I don't. It's like a snake I believe won't bite me if I simply don't get too close. I'll leave it for Randy to decide if he ever wants to share what he wrote—but I want him to be breathing when he does.

I think of all the questions I could ask. And then I think of all the answers I've buried as a wife barely breathing under a heavy blanket of self-denial.

I ignore the tears that begin to drip from my eyes as soon as I speak. "Sweetheart, I know why."

He looks up. "You do?"

"I've known for a long time. I just didn't want to believe. And maybe you've known for a long time, too—and you just didn't want to accept."

He nods and I think I've never seen him look so pained. But mixed in with his anguish, there's something else. And my best guess for what that might be is relief.

The cat's out of the bag. The door to his cell has just been opened by someone who couldn't be more dubious about granting this release.

"Was there something that gave me away? I swear to god, Vi, I've been faithful."

"I know you have, my love. And I know how hard that's been. When we're at the beach or even on the street, I see where your eyes go even though you think I'm not aware of it. I also pick up on your shame after you've looked at some hot man with longing." I stop, a little breathless. Even though I'm telling the truth, it hurts me inside. To remember my husband's lust for strange men in public places. It's not the kind of thing we want to believe, so we tell ourselves, "He's admiring that guy's haircut." Or "He likes that one's hiking boots...or his jeans...or he wonders about that car he's getting into."

Denial is an easy game to play, but one I always know—deep down—I'm cheating at.

"Aside from that, there have been a lot of little tells over the years. Your shyness, ironically, around other men." I laugh. "Your love for those old weeper movies like *Imitation of Life* or *Madame X*. I know, stereotypes.

"But I found the copy of *Gay Chicago* magazine you hid, rolled up in a sport coat. I know about that book, *The Front Runner*, that you keep in your backpack, buried under papers.

"And I know how ashamed you are. I know how much you wish you were someone else."

"You do?" He lets out a small hiccup of a sob. "I hate myself. I hear people say it's a 'lifestyle,' or it's a 'choice,' but I'm here to tell you it's not. I've been trying to unmake that 'choice' almost my whole life." He hangs his head.

I set down the champagne, and I cross to sit next to Randy on the bed. I put my arm around him and draw him close. I'm relieved because he doesn't resist. "Don't hate yourself. And don't believe the haters. Ask them when they chose to be straight and see what answer you get.

"You're a good man, no matter what you tell yourself. You're a good dad to Henry. You've been a good husband to me. No lie. Our years together have been the happiest of my life because of you. You're kind. Sweet. Sensitive. You always put everyone else first." I stare down at the carpet, a dusty rose color. I realize, in the moment, I'm putting our good, cherished time in the past.

I know we're on the brink.

"I couldn't pretend anymore," he whispers. "And if I couldn't change, well, maybe I just didn't want to be here anymore."

My response is short, but among some of the hardest words I've ever had to say. "You don't have to change or pretend. Not with me." These words are the antithesis of what I feel in my heart.

"What do you mean?" He leans back and away a little, to regard me.

She shuddered and then sighed. "I don't want you to live a lie anymore. What that means for our family?" I shrug. "I don't have a clue. But we need to figure it out. We need to see how we can all move forward." I pull the sleeping pills from my pocket and lift the bottle to show him.

He recoils at the sight, almost as though it's his first time seeing the container, when we both know it's not. His cheeks redden.

I get up, go in the adjoining bathroom, and dump the pills down the toilet. I watch as they swirl around and around when I flush. I try not to think he can simply try another way, another method. I haven't really accomplished anything, save to stave off something horrible for a moment.

When I come back, I find him stretched out on the bed, staring up at the ceiling. I lie beside him and regard the same. There's a crack running from the ceiling light fixture to a corner. Cobwebs. Crown molding that needs a dusting.

I continue to stare at the ceiling. "Don't save yourself for me. I'm a big girl. Whatever happens, I'll manage. I'll even try to be grateful for having had you. But think of Henry. He's just a little boy. Do you know what it would be like for him to grow up without you? How he may never come to grips with why his daddy didn't love him enough to stay?" I shake my head. A tear rolls down the side of my face out of the corner of my eye. "You made a son. You need to be here for him. No matter how hard that is." I try to keep the bitterness and pain out of my voice as I add, "It's not just about you anymore."

I sit up, try to soften the blow of what I just voiced. "I wanna make it easier. Okay? Can we go home and start talking? We won't stop until we come to some kind of solution. Okay?"

I feel as though I'm selling my soul to a rational devil. I feel like I'm putting my love in the path of something that will steamroll over it.

My heart is breaking, breaking, breaking—broke.

But I can't let him see. Not now. Not when he's so vulnerable.

I swallow and take a few deep calming breaths.

I stand up. It's hard for me to believe I've only been in this room for ten minutes or so. It seems like my whole life has changed in that brief span.

And it has.

But the change has been on the horizon for a long time like storm clouds gathering. I just chose not to look at them.

I go to the empty chair in the room and pick up Randy's peacoat, the bright-orange scarf he loves and I got him for Christmas. I hold them out. "Come home with me, please."

He pushes himself off the bed. Silently, he shrugs into his coat, wraps the muffler around his throat. He throws the champagne into the trash and crumples his note up and tosses it in after. He glances out the window. "It's really coming down now."

"Winter in Chicago," I say.

"Who's with Henry?" he asks as we head toward the door.

"Mrs. Roberts." She's our downstairs neighbor. She has five dogs and three cats in a one-bedroom apartment. Henry gets a huge kick out of visiting her and comes home covered in fur.

We ride the elevator to the lobby and step outside into the snow and the howling wind. We don't talk as we head toward the subway station on Chicago Avenue.

It's a good thing too. Because I don't think I *can* talk. My tears freeze, stinging, on my face.

I feel like a house made of glass.

All the supports that hold the various panes upright have just collapsed.

Chapter Four

RANDY

When we get home, I run downstairs to pick up Henry.

Mrs. Roberts, a steel-haired matron in her sixties, with a smile that belies her cold demeanor, puts a finger to her lips as she opens the door.

Henry, my cherub, slumbers on the couch, a throw pillow beneath his head and a chenille bedspread pulled up to his chin. He breathes deeply, and his cheeks still retain the fleshiness and the rosy glow from when he was a baby. His dark hair, like mine, is a curly mop spreading out onto the orange-and-white striped pillow beneath him.

The space Henry isn't taking up is occupied by animals. Two cats, a Calico called Helen and an overweight black-and-white male named AJ, are curled up on the top back of the sofa, looking comfy despite its narrowness. Two small dogs, one a chihuahua mix named Kodi and a Boston terrier called Lily, slumber near Henry's feet.

I know there are a couple other critters around here, but maybe they're hiding.

I understand hiding.

Mrs. Roberts and I don't speak as we head over to the couch. She's wearing a gentle smile as she watches me regard my son. She makes me think of my mom.

I stare down and wonder what he's dreaming about.

I feel a rush of love so intense it almost takes my breath away.

How could I have even contemplated leaving him? How could I have taken those steps?

I gently touch his soft, soft hair, then pull my hand back. A film unspools in my head—Henry calling me Daddy, his first steps, changing his diaper for the first time and getting pee on my face, his fascination with balloons, his picky eating.

My boy.

How could I have thought to leave him behind?

How could I have thought to leave Violet?

I shake my head at my selfishness. The crisis has passed. I don't know what'll happen next, but I feel sure, deep down in my bones, I won't do something as reckless as I tried to earlier today.

I smile at Mrs. Roberts and mouth "thanks" and gently reach down to gather Henry up in my arms. He wiggles and sighs but doesn't wake.

The dogs peer up at me. Kodi hops down from the couch, stretches, yawns. His curled tail wags. Lily stays put, lowering her head and falling immediately back to sleep, snoring like a truck driver.

Mrs. Roberts opens the door for me and nods. She reaches up and squeezes my shoulder. I think of what she sees—the innocence and love of a little boy and his daddy.

And then I think of what I know of myself, and the loathing rises up again. The questions come at me—why can't you just be normal? Why can't you just pretend? These are questions I've lived with on a daily basis since I was, oh, maybe twelve years old.

I've always known I was gay.

I just never accepted it. I believed I could change...

That belief was one thing that *did* die today.

I mouth a second "thanks" to Mrs. Roberts as I head out the door. She closes it softly behind me.

And I think again of what she saw and what made her smile.

A little boy and the daddy who loves him.

Despite all my self-loathing and shame, what she saw was real.

Was true.

Always.

I BEGIN TO climb the stairs. Henry is lighter than air.

As we approach, Violet opens the door. Her smile doesn't reach her eyes, which are red, the area around them puffy.

And I have to fight once more to not feel the shame, the guilt, the wish that I was someone else. She didn't ask for any of this. She only wanted to love me.

I brush by Violet and move down the hallway to Henry's room at one end. Inside, Violet has left the small lamp on his dresser illuminated, and the yellow room has a warm glow. Safe.

I reach over the edge of the barred headboard of his maple twin bed and place Henry gently on the mattress, on his back. I glance up at the mobile above his head, little stuffed VW bugs in pastel shades. When it's on, it plays "King of the Road." The music always makes Henry smile, even though he now protests he's too old for "that thing."

I keep it because it always makes me smile too.

I sometimes wonder if it will still be looking down upon him when he's in high school.

I'm grateful that my son is such a sound sleeper.

I turn off the light and close the door as I exit the room.

It's time to talk.

VIOLET AND I huddle close on the couch, wrapped in a white-and-yellow afghan my late grandmother made. It binds the two of us together in a cocoon. On the coffee table before us, an empty red wine bottle and two glasses with dark dredges in the bottom bear testimony to our long talk.

I wonder for a moment how simply talking can be so exhausting. I feel as if any energy I had in reserve has been ripped right out of me.

The sky outside our window is that indescribable gray that's more a quality of light than a color. We've passed the whole night on a magic carpet of words.

Words that made us cry. That wounded. That opened doors. Words that made us collapse into each other's arms, holding tight, pining for a dream we now know will never come true. Words that hurt. Words that angered. Truth.

They say our thoughts become words, our words become actions, and our actions become our reality.

Tonight's conversation was one of those landmark ones that will surely shape our reality going forward.

Violet is the soul of kindness, the heart of giving.

"I want you to be yourself," she tells me. "And whoever that self is, Randy, it's still *you*. And I'll always love you."

She doesn't know it, and until I hear her say the words, I didn't know either that I'd been waiting all my life for someone to tell me that. See, when you hide as I have, I question—do the people who say they love me really love me? Or do they love an ideal? A ghost image of a person who doesn't really exist?

The pain of wondering if anyone really loves you for you is real and cuts deep.

Violet has said more than she knows, and I will always be grateful for the words—words I know that come at great personal risk and sacrifice.

Violet also lays down some ground rules for us as long as we live under the same roof—neither of us knows how much longer that might be; it could be years, months, or days—we're very fragile and tenuous right now.

The first rule, which I protest by saying I'm not ready for anyone else right now, is I not bring any men home. Henry can't be confused. Violet doesn't want to meet any potential suitors. And I'm thinking that I just came out in a tiny, hurt way. Potential suitors seem like something that will be far into the future.

Despite my assurances that I have been faithful, Violet insists that I get tested for HIV and other infections. I tell her there's no way I have anything she could catch. She tells me back, "I believe you. But every lover and spouse who believed in their mate and ended up infected felt the same, I'm sure. Don't take it personally. It's just a precaution for my peace of mind."

I think of AIDS and I shudder. The stories I've read in the newspapers and magazines. It's another reason to fear "potential suitors."

Now that I know I want to live, I have to stay alive for Henry. I don't want him to visit his dad in some godforsaken AIDS ward, covered in Kaposi's Sarcoma lesions.

Rule number three is that she actually thinks I need to meet other gay people. "I'll leave it up to you how, where, and when."

She looks away when she offers this, and it makes my best friends, guilt and shame, rise up once more. I want to assure her I have no such needs, not now anyway.

But the one thing I can't bring myself to admit is that I'm hungry. Hungry to meet someone like me, not necessarily for romance or sex, but just to know there are others out there like me, maybe even other married men, so I won't feel so alone. I imagine briefly a man out there who will understand me, who will be a balm on the pain I've lived with.

I don't dare hope for someone who will make me love myself. That's going to take time, and I believe it's part of Violet's reasoning for having me make a plan to get out of my closet and meet other people.

The last thing she asks is that we never, no matter what happens, fight over Henry.

"I will never poison his mind against you. I will never try to take him away from his father. I know how much you love him."

Those words linger, and they ended our talk for this night.

Now, we watch the night morph into day.

It's a new beginning.

Almost as one, we get up from the couch and head toward our bedroom.

At the door, Vi turns to me and gives me a sad smile. She puts a hand on my chest.

"What?" I ask, already instinctively knowing, but needing confirmation.

She glances down at the floor and then back up at me, her gray eyes shining once again with tears. I wouldn't think she'd have any left. "I think I need to sleep alone. Okay?"

It breaks my heart. But I get it. I do. I'm no longer the same man she woke up next to yesterday morning—which now seems like eons ago rather than twenty-four hours.

She turns away from me and heads over to the walk-in closet. She hands me a quilt, sheet, and pillow, stacked up. "I don't know how I feel about this."

"You do." I let out a shuddering breath. "And it's okay, sweetheart. It's okay."

I turn and head back to the couch in the living room. I plop down with the bedding in my lap. Okay? I wonder if anything will ever be okay again.

Chapter Five

JOHN

Vince picks me up at nine o'clock. He calls through the intercom, "Just come on down. I'm double-parked out here, man."

The street I'm on in my neighborhood of Ravenswood, Lincoln Avenue, is a super-busy diagonal Chicago street, dotted with bars, restaurants, and specialty stores. Housing to the east of Lincoln is bigger, plusher...and a lot more expensive than my place, which sits above Wings, a Chinese restaurant that's been there so long I recall my parents calling it the "chop suey joint."

I eat way more MSG and noodles than I should, but it's too easy having a restaurant just beneath your one-bedroom.

The drawback is roaches. Roaches and restaurants in Chicago are one of the most reliable and long-lasting marriages going in the Windy City. I get the refugees from down below and am constantly in battle mode against the little critters. Their scurrying when I turn on a light in the kitchen, or even the bathroom, accounts for a lot of my stumbling around in the dark at night.

They give me the creeps.

My thoughts of Chinese cuisine and cockroaches are interrupted by Vince buzzing again.

I press the button to listen. "Dude! Get your ass down here! There's a cop car headed north, and if I get a ticket, you're gonna pay for it."

I take a quick glance at myself in the mirror—green-and-blue plaid flannel shirt, faded Levi's, a Carhartt jacket, and Asics running shoes. Cute. Manly. If I do say so myself...

I hope someone else along Halsted tonight will agree with my narcissistic assessment.

I hurry out my front door and down the flight of stairs to the street. Vince is out there in the unflattering sodium-vapor glare of a streetlight, leaning against his car, smoking a cigarette.

I hurry up to him. "Put that thing out." I pluck it from his lips and fling it to the slushy road. "You wanna kill yourself?"

I've been a paramedic with the Chicago Fire Department for the past seven years. I've loaded more smokers into the back of an ambulance than I can count. People always think of lung cancer and emphysema, but in my experience heart attacks kill more smokers than anything, whether that's borne out by evidence or not.

"What the fuck's wrong with you?" He looks longingly down at the cigarette on the ground, only a quarter smoked. "Do you know how expensive those are these days?"

I get in the passenger seat and look over at him, pointedly. "Do you know how expensive a funeral is these days?" I grin. "Oh right, you do, Mr. Funeral Director."

We head off just as the cop car is drawing near.

"Sidetrack?" Vince asks.

"Comedy night. It's our Thursday tradition."

SIDETRACK, NOT SURPRISINGLY, is packed wall-to-wall with gay boys, curious straight girls, and assorted folks caught in the middle. It's a video bar and one of the most popular along the Halsted strip of gay establishments. I suspect that has something to do with the videos, which run constantly. If you're a lonely guy out by yourself, having something to watch on multiple screens around the space gives you something to do.

It also helps that the bar must have a policy about hiring only the cutest men on the planet to bartend.

Comedy night is my favorite, though. The only time more popular is show tunes on Sundays, but I've never been into musicals. I'm always waiting for the singing to be over, like a commercial, so we can get back to the story.

I know, take away my gay card.

But I love all the old clips Sidetrack manages to gather for their comedy event—*Golden Girls, America's Funniest Home Videos, Designing Women*, to name a few. There's also footage from scores of comedy movies going back to the 1930s. Stand-up comics too.

And if you're like Vince, who smoked a joint in the car before we got out, the clips are even more hysterical. He always urges me to partake, and I'd love to say yes, but I get drug tested at my job regularly.

And I love my job. So I just say no.

Vince buys our first round of Bud Lights while I grab some wall space for the two of us. I watch him maneuver through the crowd. He's tall, blond, blue-eyed. J Crew model all the way. Mine are not the only eyes following him in his tight jeans and form-fitting white V-neck cashmere sweater.

I wish I could love him. We get along great. And, judging by the swiveling heads and flirtatious stares as he passes, I couldn't do a whole lot better in the looks department. He's harbored a not-so-secret crush on me for years.

A relationship with Vince Parker would be so easy, effortless. We'd look good together—I'd be yin to his yang. Dark and light. Complementary.

But. But.

There's simply no spark. As much as it would make sense for Vince and I to be a couple, it simply can't happen. I *need* that spark—to feel that indescribable *something* that makes songwriters and artists swoon over the power of real love.

I don't know if I'll ever find it. It's elusive. And so far, I've kissed a lot of frogs and turned over a lot of stones in my search, but never seem to be able to capture what might pass for the fireworks of true love.

Honestly—and I've thought a lot about this—I'd rather be alone, than settle.

Vince steps up beside me and hands me a brown bottle. I clink the top of it against his and thank him.

He scans the crowd. "See anything you like? Any prospects?"

I look over the room. Guys are standing practically shoulder-to-shoulder and most of them are young and cute. Above them, on several screens, there's a vintage clip from the old *Laugh-In* TV show. I remember it vaguely from my childhood. Right now, Lily Tomlin's doing her Ernestine the Telephone Operator shtick and people are mostly glued to it, howling with laughter.

A haze of blue-gray smoke rises above everyone and hovers near the ceiling. I hate how I know my clothes will smell when I get home.

Vince lights up to join in the fog of tobacco smoke, and I scowl at him.

"Oh, grow up." He blows smoke at me, and I wave it away.

I shrug in answer to his question about prospects. Although there's a cute redhead with a beard ordering at the bar, I can clearly see he's with the guy next to him, a hot daddy with a close-cropped salt-and-pepper beard and shaved head. Judging from the way their muscles push out their tight white T-shirts—with the sleeves turned up even more to show off the guns, naturally—they spend most of their lives at the gym. "I don't really see anyone, but hey, the night is young."

Vince shakes his head and smiles at me. "No one is ever good enough for you."

I smile back and have to wonder if he includes himself in that group. I hope not. I love Vince with all my heart—but all it will ever be, all it's *ever* been, for me, is as a friend.

Imagining Vince and I together sexually or romantically simply seems like incest.

Yuck.

Vince says, "Well, I see a guy I met over the weekend at Touché standing back there. Total top with a thing for blonds." He gestures with his beer bottle toward a beefy, bearded guy with dark skin, black hair, and what looks like a surly scowl permanently affixed to his face. Despite this, Vince says, "You don't mind if I go say hello, do you?"

I remind him we're not on a date. "Law of the jungle applies here." We have an agreement that all bets are off as to the future of our evening out together if either of us meets a hot guy.

"I'll be right back." Vince leaves me alone.

"Sure you will." I know Vince doesn't even hear my reply. My beer bottle has only a splash left in the bottom, and I'm thinking about heading over to the bar for another one, maybe grab a shot of Jack to go with it this time, when I see *him.*

He's just come in and he's scared shitless. Even from across the bar, the fear in his face is plain—the restless way his eyes scan the crowd, as though they're all predators and he's bleeding. He shrinks against the wall, just shy of cringing.

I feel for him. It must be not only his first time here, but also his first time in a gay bar, despite his age, which I would estimate early thirties. It wasn't all that long ago I was in his shoes. Sure, I was out. But only to Vince, a girl friend (note: two words) who lives in the apartment above mine, and my priest.

Yes, I'm a Catholic boy. Irish Catholic, the worst—or the best—kind, depending on your perspective.

But I, too, until about two years ago, was afraid to set foot in any kind of gay establishment. In fact, I lost my virginity to a guy I met in a *straight* bar on Rush Street when I was twenty-two. It took Vince a lot of coaxing to get me to go into a gay bar. I was afraid one of the firefighters from my station might see me (never mind what *he* was doing in the same place or even on Halsted, the heart of Chicago's Boystown).

So, I recognize and empathize with the fear on this guy's face. The way he's holding his arms over his chest. The tightness in his body as though he's coiled, ready to sprint at the slightest provocation. His shoulders are drawn up close to his ears. For someone in a place where people come to party and socialize, he seems pretty miserable.

It's a shame, too, because his fear eclipses just how adorable he is. Or maybe he's adorable to me because he's so obviously terrified. That might sound weird, but you have to understand—I have a nurturing streak a mile wide. It's a big part of why I became a paramedic.

He's got wavy dark brown or maybe even black hair, brushed back away from his face and covering the tops of his ears. A five-o-clock shadow defines, rather than hides, the dimples and the sharp jawline. His eyes, even through the haze and the dimness, look dark, almost black. He's got this big mustache. I know Vince would call it a porn star 'stache, but it's a huge turn-on for me, perhaps precisely because it *is* vintage porn star. I love those old movies with hunks like Jon King, Al Parker, and Chad Douglas. Maybe it's why I didn't come out sooner—my VCR satisfied my cravings.

Anyway, this guy would fit right in with those hunky, hairy men who populated the old movies like *Boys in the Sand, El Paso Wrecking Company*, and my all-time favorite, *LA Tool and Die*.

As I move to the bar, I check to see if he has a drink. His hands are empty. I wonder if he'd like a beer? Ah, I'll get him one. It can be an icebreaker. And if he doesn't like beer, I do. So it won't go to waste. I'll get him whatever he wants.

Because... Because he's cute. Sexy. Masculine. Because you always remember the kindness of strangers. I don't know him yet, but I like to think there's a potential for sparks here. And I can't resist being a friendly face and welcoming voice when I can tell he's extremely uncomfortable.

At the very least, I hope it will knock his discomfort down a notch or two. At the most, maybe he'll be that elusive connection I'm always seeking.

When I first started going out, I at least had Vince to lean on. This guy seems to have no one. He might as well be wearing a T-shirt with LONER emblazoned across its front.

At the bar, I order two bottles of Bud Light. Just as the bartender sets them down in front of me with a wink and a ripple of his serpent-tattooed bicep, the redhead and the daddy step up to me.

"Hey, handsome. Don't think I've seen you out before," the redhead says. He's all smiles. He touches my hand for a moment.

Before I can stop him, the daddy's paying for my beers. He tells the bartender, whom he calls Cole, to keep the change. Cole gives him the same lascivious wink he just threw my way. I have a feeling Cole's wink is given out pretty indiscriminately...all for a two-dollar tip.

I glance over at where the scared mustache stood and, to my disappointment, see he's no longer there. Bummer. I turn my head to look through the crowd, hoping to spy him, but all I see, of note, is Vince in a corner, already making out with his beefy friend from over the weekend. I guess I'll be taking the L home.

"You new?"

"What?" I turn to the daddy, giving him my attention. I notice his eyes are a little bloodshot. He seems a bit too eager, and it puts me off.

"Just wonder why we never noticed a sexy dude like you here before." The daddy smiles and takes a swig of beer. He's hot, but in a kind of hard, polished way, like he works too hard at it. In my book, the sexiest guys are the ones who are least aware of it.

His redhead buddy—lover?—chimes in, "You from out of town?"

"Huh? No. Born and raised in Chicago. Grew up in Berwyn and live up in Ravenswood now, by Lincoln Square." I keep scanning the crowd, hoping my guy will appear again, that he's only gone to the men's room and not out the exit door.

"You looking for someone?" The redhead raises one eyebrow, as though to say, "Could that someone be me…or us?"

I take a swig from my beer and raise it to them. "Thanks for this." Then I answer the redhead. "I thought I saw a friend in the crowd, that's all." I try to peer at all the clustered bodies again, looking for that amazing mustache, but I still don't see him.

The redhead extends a hand. "I'm Marc."

I shake his hand but don't feel I'm really present. "John."

Marc says, "This is my boyfriend, Craig."

I shake his hand too. I'm still searching for the guy I saw earlier, hoping he's returned from the men's room, hoping he'll sidle up next to me to get himself a drink. I barely hear one of the guys tell me, "We think you're hot."

"Thanks, guys." I manage. "You're hot too. Really." *And any other time, I might be interested in exploring this hotness with you, but I'm a little distracted right now.*

Craig leans in close. "We were just gonna head home, actually. We live right around the corner on Roscoe. You wanna come over? We have party favors, and the sling is all set up."

"Whoa!" I say, not bothering to try to hide my surprise. "Uh, I just got here. But, uh, thanks for the invite. Maybe another time?"

"Sure thing," Marc says.

Both of them are already turning away, hungry, I suppose, for their next prospect—a more willing one than I am. I'm sure they won't have any trouble. But I can't help but feel sorry for them. They're together, but here they are, out on the prowl. Maybe it works for them. Who knows?

But that kind of thing would never play in my world. When, and if, I ever find a guy I want to be with in a more permanent way, we won't be out, hunting for a third. To each his own, but their forwardness and the naked hunger in the couple's eyes smacks of desperation.

Maybe I'm just a hopeless romantic.

I grab my other bottle from the bar. "Catch you later." I raise my bottle to the backs of their retreating heads.

I shoulder my way through the crowd, praying I'll see the guy again. The fact that I saw him and lost him makes him seem like more of a prize than he actually is, but so be it.

If I don't find him, I might just be ready to head home. Especially since I can't see Vince anywhere either. I figure he and the "total top" are on their way to one of their places, or maybe Vince has him in one of the stalls in the men's room.

It wouldn't be the first time.

I get across the bar and set my two bottles on a little shelf. I lean back against the wall. There's a clip playing of the coyote pursuing the roadrunner that makes me think of the encounter I just had at the bar.

Damn those guys for distracting me!

But...wait a minute.

Maybe it's not too late.

I see him coming toward me from the direction of the men's room at the back. He looks no less sexy. And no less scared. His eyes are fixed on the door out to Halsted.

Which makes me think—now or never.

I lean forward as he nears me. "Don't I know you?"

"What?" He eyes me suspiciously. His voice has the tiniest flutter of panic in it. He glances behind himself, presumably to make sure I'm addressing him.

"Yeah, weren't you in that movie?" I grin.

"What movie?"

Vince and I have this little thing where we go up to strange men we want to meet and ask if they were in "that movie." When they ask which one, one or the other of us says, "My Ass and Your Face." But I fear such a response would send my mustachioed friend screaming into the night.

So I try something a little tamer, not much, but a little. I so need to get a smile out of this character. My new life mission is to take away a little of the obvious unease he's feeling. So I blurt, "Aren't you Al Parker?" I lean a little closer and that proximity nearly takes my breath away. I peer into his eyes. "You are, aren't you? I was just enjoying your performance in *The Other Side of Aspen* last night."

He looks totally befuddled—and no less uneasy. "I don't know what you're talking about."

I believe him. There's something naïve practically radiating off him. I shrug, feeling foolish. "It's a movie. I was just kidding." I turn and grab the extra beer off the shelf and hold it out to him. "Sorry. I'm not too good at opening lines, obviously." I press the beer close to his hand. "You wanna beer? You look thirsty."

He looks down at it and moves his hand back. "I'm okay. So what kind of movie is this *Other Side of Aspen*?"

Now I'm sorry I tried this gambit. Anybody else in the bar probably would have picked up on the reference—and been flattered as hell.

But not this one. And I sort of admire him for it. Have I just run across the last innocent gay man in Chicago?

And is he open to being corrupted? *Shut your filthy mind, John!*

"It's porn," I explain.

He looks a little taken aback. And he still hasn't taken the beer from me.

"A porn? Like gay porn?" He cocks his head. He doesn't look offended, just confused.

"Is there any other kind?" I ask.

Ah, there it is. A tiny smile. I made him smile. I feel like doing a happy dance.

"You thought I was in a porno?"

"Nah. As I said, I thought it was a good opening line. Maybe I should have just said, "Hi, my name is John. And who might you be?"

He eyes me, a little smirk lifting up the corners of his lips. "Randy."

I reach out to shake his hand and realize I still have the beer I offered him. He takes it from me and drinks a long swallow.

"Nice to meet you. You come here a lot?"

He looks around the place with an expression I can only read as *How the hell did I get here?* He shakes his head and takes another long swallow. I notice he's drained the bottle in two gulps. *What a man!*

I point to the empty bottle. "You want another one?" I feel like I've neared a shy animal, and one false move could send him running.

Apparently, my offer of that second beer was that one false move. "No." He sets the bottle on the shelf. "Um, nice meeting you. But I gotta go." He starts away.

"You have to leave so soon?" I try to keep the whine out of my voice.

He looks back at me, and I swear there are tears in his eyes. He blinks once, twice, and his face returns to that of a scared jackrabbit.

"I have to go." And with that, he's gone.

I have to restrain myself from giving chase as he hurries out the door. I know I'd only scare him more if I took off after him.

I finish my beer and take in the crowd once more. I feel removed from the drinking, the flirting, and the laughter. Vince is still nowhere in sight. The couple who hit on me earlier are chatting up some young kid with a thick mane of curly blond hair, who looks barely old enough to be in here. But I can see he's all kinds of eager.

I have two choices.

I can stay and get drunk, maybe bleary-eyed enough to find a halfway acceptable stranger to take home.

Or I can just go home.

I choose the latter. Maybe I'll crawl into bed and pop *The Other Side of Aspen* into the VCR. And dream of Randy...

Chapter Six

RANDY

I stand outside the bar, trembling. It's cold out here, with a wind blowing off the lake a few blocks to the east. There's even a few snowflakes dancing in the air.

But that's not why I'm shaking. No, that comes from crossing a line I'd never been able to cross before—actually going into a gay bar. I've snuck home copies of the gay rags, *Gay Chicago* and *Outlines*, and studied them when Violet was asleep or gone to visit her family in Lake Forest. I knew the names of all the places on Halsted, like Sidetrack, Roscoe's, Little Jim's, Christopher Street, and even the bars farther south, down near the intersection of Grand and Clark. I've gazed hungrily at the ads, wondering what it would be like to have the freedom to get myself dressed to go out and then actually going and being part of the crowd.

I've fantasized meeting a special guy. Flirtatious smiles from across a crowded dance floor. The gay equivalent of Tony and Maria in the dance scene in *West Side Story* where they first meet.

But which one would I be?

I picked Sidetrack because *Gay Chicago* had mentioned Thursday was comedy night, and I thought, for my first outing, something that would distract me and the people around me would be just the ticket. I felt maybe I could vanish into a laughing crowd.

But it didn't work out that way. People kept looking at me, and I wondered if there was something amiss: my fly was unzipped or my chamois shirt was buttoned wrong. Untied shoelace?

I simply wanted to stand and observe, maybe get a little glimpse into this world that had always attracted and repelled me.

I never dared think guys were looking at me because they found me attractive. It was more a belief they were laughing at me and immediately spotted the outsider, the one who didn't fit in, the one who could never belong.

It felt as though my whole skin was tingling. It sounds narcissistic—and it is—but I imagined everyone was staring at me (and deep inside, laughing at the nebbish guy hugging the wall).

I thought of Violet, earlier that evening at home, watching me as I got ready. God bless her, she was trying to be encouraging, but I could see the hurt vulnerability in her face. I even offered to stay home. But we'd discussed my meeting other gay people. I'm sure it wasn't true, but we both felt that neither of us knew any.

I'd asked her why she was allowing this. What wife urges her husband to get out to meet other gay men?

"Because I don't love a gay man, I love *you*," she told me. "This isn't easy for me. But I never want to see you sink as low as that day I found you at that hotel downtown. Gay, straight, bi, or whatever—I want you around. Henry wants you around. And he needs you around. Being gay doesn't stand in the way of you being the wonderful, loving father he's known since he was born."

I'd been both touched and hurt by her words. How did I get so lucky? The old self-loathing crept in, and I thought I should redouble my efforts to at least live a life that was, to all appearances, a straight one.

And yet, I knew I just couldn't do it. Not now, when I'd removed the mask, when she'd shown me that me being myself didn't have to mean being some twisted, broken thing, but a person she continued to love.

A good person.

So, I'd found comedy night and Sidetrack and decided to try that first. Maybe things like this aren't supposed to work out the first time. Maybe a bar was the wrong choice. Perhaps a gay church, like the Metropolitan Community Church, which I'd also read about in one of the gay rags, would be more my speed.

Now, I find myself walking up Halsted under the bright streetlights, huddling into my peacoat, still shivering. Guys pass me, at ease, laughing and talking, and I wonder how they pull off that trick. Had they always been accepting of themselves? Was I in the minority of the minority—hating myself, wanting desperately to change what some fools considered a choice?

Some of the guys swivel their heads as they watch me go by. I should be flattered, but their scrutiny and attraction makes me almost nauseous, violated. I never return the stares, but I can feel them boring into the back of my head.

And that guy at the bar! What was up with him? I don't know. Did he really want to meet me? Or was he, too, making fun of an obviously scared guy who felt out of place?

It's hard for me to believe he had any kind of malicious intent. In spite of how I beat myself up, it was pretty obvious he was just trying to be nice, to do the right thing.

Did he think I was cute? Was he trying to pick me up?

Who knows? I'm not fluent in this language yet, and I can't discern the mating calls of gay men. I suppose, just like in the straight world, walking up to someone in a bar, chatting with them, and offering them a drink is a way of showing interest, right?

There's a little diner just east of Halsted on Addison. Its bright lights and intimation of warmth draw me inside. There's a clock over the counter, and it tells me that it's twenty after ten. At this hour, the place is relatively empty, still waiting, I suppose, for the late-night rush when the bars are closing and folks are seeking a little sustenance before heading home.

I stamp the snow off my feet as I stand in the doorway and take in the place. It could be a diner anywhere in the Midwest, probably in America, really. It has too-bright lighting, black-and-white checked tile floors, a chrome-and-red Formica counter, behind which I can see the short order cook: a guy with a pot belly, bald pate, and a stained white apron. He's flipping burgers and has a pile of onions caramelizing. Those, at least, smell amazing and make my mouth water. There's also a soda fountain and other appliances back there where the food magic happens.

Opposite the counter is a row of red leatherette booths with chrome and Formica tables that match the counter. Each booth has its own wall sconce light fixture and jukebox.

There's a couple of older men at the counter with pie and coffee in front of them. Their heads, both gray, are pressed close as they talk and laugh. One wears a red buffalo-plaid shirt and faded jeans and the other, heavyset, is wearing some blousy silk shirt with black pants that almost look like tights. I wonder if they're a couple. Have they been together for many years? What have they seen? Do they remember things like bar raids, having to be buzzed into gay establishments at the door, cruising guys under the big clock at Marshall Field's downtown?

Part of me wants to sidle up to them, eavesdrop, or maybe even join in their conversation. Maybe they've been through what I have, even been married, and will have some sage words for me.

My thoughts are interrupted by the arrival of a waitress, dressed in a pink polyester dress with a white apron over it. She looks to be at least seventy, with brassy, dyed-orange hair and matching lipstick. Her face is lined heavily, but her smile, which deepens all the lines, is tired but warm.

"Hi, hon. You want a booth, or you wanna belly up to the counter?"

I almost say, "I'll take the counter," so I can sit next to what I'm guessing is the gay couple already there. But I've been conspicuous enough for one night. "A booth."

She grabs a menu from a stack at the hostess desk and leads me to the farthest booth in the back, which I like because I can finally observe without being observed back too much.

Other than the gay couple, the only other customer is a woman at another booth a couple of tables away. She's young, maybe only in her teens, with dyed-black hair, wearing a belted plaid coat and ear muffs. I wonder why she doesn't take off her outer garments. Isn't she hot?

I sit and watch her eat her cheeseburger. She takes a bite, chews, and then spits the chewed meat into a coffee cup.

I shudder.

Nauseated, I take my gaze away and direct it toward the menu. I peruse its long list of offerings. I haven't eaten since lunch, and I'm suddenly hungry.

The waitress returns, and I see by her name tag that she's Virginia. I wonder what kind of life she's led, why she's still on her feet in a cheap diner at going on eleven o'clock on a weeknight. Can't she retire?

"What can I get you?"

"Tea? And maybe the hot meatloaf sandwich?"

"That comes with a side, along with the mashed potatoes and gravy."

I glance down at the menu again and order coleslaw. She jots down my order and starts away.

"Virginia?"

She turns and smiles. "Yup?"

"Can I, uh, have French fries instead of the mashed?"

"You got it."

"And can you put gravy on the fries?"

She laughs. "You're a boy after my own heart. I'm on it. Anything to drink?"

"A cherry Coke?"

"Coming right up."

I sit back in the booth, thinking how surreal it is that I'm here in this nearly empty diner on a Thursday night as the snow outside begins to come down more heavily. I feel as though I've been misplaced. A voice, suspiciously like my mom's, back in East Liverpool, Ohio, pops up, "You're a married man. You belong at home with your wife and son. You need to patch things up, Randy."

"Right, Mom." I whisper and then stop when I realize I'm speaking out loud. *This coming from a woman whose husband is at the American Legion or VFW every night of the week.*

Still, my mom is Italian and she raised me with plenty of Roman Catholic guilt, so I wince at her words, even if they're only imaginary.

The meatloaf sandwich comes, the anorectic girl leaves, and I dig in. The meatloaf is delicious, with big chunks of onion and green pepper. The brown gravy is deliciously salty. And the fries are actually hand cut with the skin still on, crispy on the outside and delightfully soft inside.

If nothing else, this meatloaf sandwich and fries will make the night a win.

I'm just about finished and looking around for Virginia, so I can get my check, when they come in.

It must be a gaggle of refugees from the bars. There are five of them, and they all crowd into the booth next to me before anyone even approaches them about seating. They're an odd assortment of black, white, young, old, fat, and thin.

The one thing they do have in common is they're all gay. I don't mean to stereotype, but they're all just one tiara shy of mounting the stage at the local drag show. From dyed platinum-blond hair to red-polished fingernails to assorted rhinestone brooches and dangling earrings, these guys are not, unlike me for most of my life, trying to hide anything about themselves. They're out and proud, as the talk goes. No apologies. Take-no-prisoners homos.

I study them like creatures at the Lincoln Park Zoo. One of them notices me, a guy about my own age, in tight jeans, a distressed leather bomber jacket, and a wifebeater T-shirt way too cold for this weather. In spite of the macho clothes, he's wearing eyeliner and mascara. He leers at me and makes a little kissing expression.

I stare furiously down at my plate, the smears of gravy and now-limp fries. My face burns.

I don't look up, but I can't help but overhear. They're all screaming at once. Shrieking. Except for one guy, who sounds like James Earl Jones, they all have high, women's voices. Whether they cultivated them or were born with them, I can't say.

But the honest truth is they make me cringe.

They make me feel even more like I don't belong here in Boystown. That I don't belong among gay folks.

But if I'm not one of them, where do I fit in, now that I've laid down the sword and the shield and stopped fighting who I really am?

And their talk! It's filthy—they have no compunction about discussing their sexual escapades. "Honey, his dick was as big around as a beer can and about eight inches long," one of them said, pausing for effect. The effect it had on me was to make me feel simultaneously sick, while at the same time, my dick stirred in my pants. And then he went on to tell his friends, "And the fucker turned out to be a bottom!"

The table explodes into laughter.

"I told him, 'Girl, I ordered sausage.'"

More shrieking laughter.

"What did you do? What did you do?"

"Well, I had to let him blow me, at least." Then, petulantly, he said, "But I'm still hungry for some semen, you know?"

I wondered if they were doing this for my benefit. I wondered if they could see how red my face must be. I wondered myself. My face felt like it was on fire.

I got up, hoping the bulge in my crotch wasn't showing. I headed for the cash register, and one of them wolf whistled as I passed by.

"Girlfriend, there's your top," one cried out. "Wedding ring and all!" The entire table exploded with laughter.

I glanced down at my left hand and thought how observant they were.

At the register, I wait for Virginia to make her way across the checked floor. I notice she has a little limp, and I try to be patient. This time, I don't think it's my imagination that I'm being stared at. Voices are blessedly lowered, but I can't help but feel I'm being mocked. I've entered an upside-down world.

She says softly, "Sorry about them."

I shake my head as I grope for my wallet. I have to lift my coat to grab it and one of them screams, "Be still my heart! That ass!"

"I thought you were a bottom," one replies.

"I can still appreciate a nice tushie!"

Virginia rolls her eyes, but I can see a laugh is playing at the corners of her lips.

"They're here several nights a week. Shameless. But amusing. And there's no quieting them. Once upon a time, I made the mistake of trying."

"They're okay," I say.

"They are. Good tippers."

She looks around in her little leatherette folder for my check. She brings it out and hands it to me. "Everything okay, sweetie?"

For a moment, I think she's asking in general. I want to tell her that my marriage is falling apart, I have a little boy that I love, and I was testing the waters tonight to see how I fit in with my people, but now I'm really scared, wondering if I fit in neither the gay nor the straight world. And then it dawns on me she's asking about my meal.

"Everything was delicious. Those fries!" I smile.

"They are good, aren't they? I can't eat them anymore because of the old ticker, but I remember. Al soaks them in ice water before he fries them." She rings me up and holds my change out.

"Keep it," I say.

"Good night!" The guys at the table next to mine call out as I approach the door.

I turn and know my smile looks more like a grimace.

"It's okay, honey," the blond who flirted with me earlier says. "We don't bite." He waits for a second and then adds, "Much."

Their laughter follows me out of the restaurant.

I walk all the way to the L stop near Wrigley Field with my ears burning in spite of the cold.

On the platform, as I await the next northbound train, I wonder if there's anywhere I'll ever fit in.

Because, right now, I'm more of an outsider than ever.

I can't wait to get home to where things are safe—with my wife or son.

I know they say being gay isn't a choice. But it's my choice if I have to live the life.

I suppose those guys in the diner were harmless and they were just having a good time, a night out.

But I felt like I was standing with my nose pressed against the glass of a window, looking in at a place I could never be comfortable in.

And it made me sick.

I shut down my thinking as the train rolls into the station.

1986, Spring

From "The Wasteland"
*April is the cruellest month, breeding
Lilacs out of the dead land, mixing
Memory and desire, stirring
Dull roots with spring rain.
Winter kept us warm, covering
Earth in forgetful snow, feeding
A little life with dried tubers.*
—T.S. Eliot

Chapter Seven

JOHN

I play the answering-machine message back one more time. I don't know whether to laugh or cry. Or just wince from the sting...

"John, thanks for nothing. Listen, here's the sound of me tearing up your number. I never want to hear from you or see you again. Prick." And this is followed by the very effective sound effect of paper being ripped into a million tiny little pieces, one matching each fragment from Dean Corvello's broken heart.

The message makes me want to laugh.

The message makes me want to cry.

The message makes me want to give up on men.

Maybe I should try women? It would sure as hell make my mom happy if I did. Maybe I should join the priesthood. It would make my dad happy if I did. And it might make a lot of priests drop to their knees in gratitude if they saw me walk into the sacristy. Hush. I never said that!

Dean Corvello was my latest adventure in seeking true love and coming up empty-handed.

What did I expect? We met in the sleazy back room of a leather bar a few blocks west of the Halsted Boystown strip. While patrons just a few feet away were downing bottled beer, watching hardcore porn, and playing pool, the backroom on that particular Saturday night was standing room only—a claustrophobe's nightmare and a hedonist's dream come true.

There's no pretty way to describe how Dean and I met. The bald, down-and-dirty truth is I was leaning against the wall in said backroom, drinking my Bud Light and watching as shadows moved in the near-pitch darkness, coupling, uncoupling, moaning, and groaning. A guy just across from me was bent over, jeans around his ankles, pulling a train. And we are not talking Lionel here.

Other assorted characters were involved in much the same kind of activity—anal, oral, manual for the wussies.

The floor was covered with enough DNA to populate a small country.

There was very little kissing! This wasn't your mama's old-fashioned Harlequin romance, kids.

Dean Corvello was stealthy.

Without even so much as a how-do-you-do, he hunkered down on his knees in front of me. Quickly, with no glance upward and certainly no request for permission, he unbuttoned my Levi 501s and yanked them down to my thighs.

I looked down and through the darkness could see a bearish young man, dressed in a leather harness, jeans, and combat boots. He had a shock of dark hair, buzzed close on the sides and a full beard.

Now, before you go thinking this was a sexual assault, let me disabuse you of that notion. What Dean and I were beginning to engage in was simply par for the course for the backroom of a sleazy bar in Chicago. You didn't step into one thinking you might find a partner with whom to share a spirited game of Parcheesi and a bowl of chocolate ice cream.

I was already excited because of the live sex shows going on all around me, so I didn't object when he took my cock in his mouth in a way that reminded me of a cow lowering its head to graze.

We had yet to say a word (his mom raised him right—you don't talk with your mouth full) as Dean got busy on my stiff and twitching member, sliding up and down, swirling his tongue around the shaft, moving away to lave and bite gently at my balls. I threaded my fingers through his thick, dark hair.

With his ministrations and all that was going on around me, I didn't have the heart to stop him to make proper introductions. No, I simply quietly sipped my beer and blissed out on what a perfect stranger was happy to do, unrequested, for me in a bar on a Thursday night.

You have to admit, sometimes being gay does have its perks. Especially since I came into this bar with the objective of leaving it one load lighter.

Earlier tonight, I was fixed up with a hair colorist named Troy from Lincoln Park who was all over me, yet couldn't seem to remember my name, even though I'd told it to him at least three times. We'd had dinner and he'd brought a coupon, which he applied to his meal, leaving me to pay the full price for mine. The last straw was when he admitted, as so many of the guys I seem to run into admit eventually, that he was already in a relationship, not with one, but two guys, but they were in a bad place, and he "didn't think" they'd be able to work things out.

At least Dean down there, bobbing away, had an excuse for not knowing my name was John. I tried not to wonder if I was the first guy he'd provided his top-notch service to tonight, or if I was the tenth (hey, it happens every night in this very back room—don't look so shocked). And if I was the tenth, or the hundredth, that he wasn't smearing my dick with the clap or worse.

Funny how his mouth and tongue and his desperate groaning as he chowed down on me like a prisoner getting his last meal made me forget my worries about propriety and infection and let out my own moan (muffled—I didn't want to attract attention; unlike some of the guys in this backroom, I was not an exhibitionist, despite current evidence to the contrary) as I unloaded. I had whispered, just before things reached, um, a head, "I'm gonna come." It was the polite thing to do, allowing him to pull away if he didn't want to swallow, but all it caused him to do was double down on his efforts.

After I shot and Dean had played out a Maxwell House coffee commercial, making sure that I was indeed "good to the last drop," he rose up on his feet to look me in the eye. He wiped a drop of my come (at least I think it was mine) from his mustache and grinned.

"Thanks," he said.

"I should be the one thanking you," I whispered. "That was incredible."

"I'm good at my work."

"You certainly are."

Not only was he cute in a beefy, burly sort of way (kind of like me), he seemed to have a sense of humor as well. So, while my standard modus operandi in a situation like this one would have been to make a hurried exit not only from the backroom, but from the bar itself, I changed my mind that night.

"Buy you a beer?" I asked him.

The smile that lit up his face was way out of proportion to my offer. You'd think I'd said "Buy you a Maserati?" instead of a lousy beer.

We headed out of the backroom, not holding hands, but more of a couple than when we'd gone in separately and alone earlier. Guys seldom emerge from the backroom in pairs.

At the bar, Dean said, "No one's ever done this before."

I handed him his beer and asked, "Come in your mouth?"

He laughed and clinked his beer bottle against mine. "No. I mean, offered to buy me a drink after I blew them."

"Well, you earned it."

"Right? So why don't any of these fools understand that it might be nice to offer me something to drink, other than their man juice, after getting their nut courtesy of yours truly?"

"You got me." I extended my hand. "John."

He shook it. "Dean."

Now, you'd think, after a start like that, we'd be on our way to white picket fences and a house in Naperville, with a pair of miniature schnauzers we'd call Abbott and Costello.

Not that night, but Dean quickly wore out his welcome.

Now, I found myself erasing his bitter, but oddly amusing message from my answering machine. I didn't need to hear it another time to get his point.

I lay back on my bed and replayed my brief relationship with Dean.

We'd exchanged numbers that night, even though I had offered to bring Dean home to my place. I was still a little horny and, even if I wasn't, I figured I could return his favor and not sleep alone for a change.

That's when the number exchange came in, because Dean told me, "I'm not quite ready to leave yet."

"Oh?" I asked.

He swallowed his beer a little too fast and choked for a moment.

"I didn't think you were capable of choking. Or gagging," I said.

"Even superheroes have their off moments."

I nodded. "Well, I need to head home." I couldn't admit it to him, because it would make me seem like a prude (but only in this environment), but I was a little put off by the fact that he'd rather stay than go home with me.

That should have been red flag number one.

I not so kiddingly said, "Try not to stay out too late, boy. You need your rest."

He grinned at me, and I noticed how his gaze wandered back to the entrance of the backroom. "Yes, Dad."

I leaned in to give him a peck on the lips. "I'll call you, okay?"

I had no choice, then, but to walk away. I hoped Dean was staying because he'd arranged to meet a friend or was in line to play the winner at the pool table, or even because his favorite scene was coming up from the porno playing on the big screen.

I hurried up the stairs to the main bar and dance floor, where things were a little more innocent.

I stopped at the door. The bouncer looked at me. "Forget something?"

"Yeah, my penicillin shot."

He chuckled.

I hated myself for doing it, and thought I was already being jealous and over-possessive of a guy I honestly barely knew, but I headed halfway down the stairs to look over the bar down there.

Dean was nowhere in sight.

Now, he could have been in the men's room. It was possible, although unlikely, because he almost certainly would have passed me since the restroom was upstairs and I'd barely been out of his sight for more than a couple of minutes.

I turned around, mentally kicking myself, and trying to banish from my mind the image of him again in the backroom, milking a load with his mouth on some other guy.

I had to fight an internal battle to not go in the backroom once more and check up on him. If he was back there on his knees, I didn't really want to see. It was way too soon to be so possessive and so suspicious.

I did call him the next day, and we went out to dinner the following Friday. It wasn't a bad date. We went to a near north side Italian place that was too expensive but really good and got to know each other. Dean worked for a supermarket chain that had locations all over Chicagoland, Jewel (or *the* Jewel as we locals called it) and was a butcher. He did seem to know his meat. I liked that he was a simple guy and hardworking. No pretense.

I didn't like that he was a heavy smoker.

Red flag number two.

And that he refused to sit in the nonsmoking section of the restaurant to make me happy.

When we went home, he was a total bottom, and I fucked him, safely of course, although he told me he'd just been tested and was "clean," by which he meant that I could toss that rubber aside.

Uh-uh. I opted to keep it on. "Just in case," I told him tenderly, as I thrust hard into him.

Red flag number three—doesn't play safe.

And that remark about being clean? Um, without getting too gross here (and I know he meant being free of disease by clean), but he wasn't really all that clean, judging from the skid marks he left on my sheets.

Red flag number four—if you're a bottom and you like to get fucked, you need to make sure that hole is squeaky clean.

After he left in the morning, and I was washing my sheets in the laundry in the basement of my building, I excused him by telling myself that maybe he tried to clean himself out properly, but sometimes you missed a spot. Accidents happen.

Shit happens.

The next date was for breakfast at Ann Sather the following Sunday. I was coming down with a cold, so I asked if he wouldn't mind if we'd sit in the nonsmoking section.

He refused.

Really? I was coughing and sniffling. What was more important? Me or the cancer sticks? Wait, don't answer that. I knew if I asked out loud, the answer was clear, and I didn't want to face that I'd lose out to a fucking cigarette.

We had an okay breakfast, but after paying my half of the bill (plus a little extra because my eggs Benedict cost more than his French toast), I told him I needed to get over to my mom and dad's for early Sunday corned beef and cabbage.

It was all a lie. I had no such tradition with my parents even if they were hardcore South Side Black Irish.

But I needed to get away from Dean and the images I couldn't remove from my head, not the least of which was a Marlboro Light extinguished into a slice of half-eaten French toast. Dean may have lost his gag reflex, but I hadn't, and just conjuring up that image made my skin crawl and the bile rise.

In the end, I did what I despised other gay men for doing to me in the past—and that I cursed them for—I simply stopped calling him and, worse, didn't return his calls, which got more and more frequent the less inclined I was to answer them.

His latest answering machine message, I hoped, was the last I'd hear from Dean.

Didn't he get that no response was a response?

I thought about throwing on some clothes and going out tonight. Vince had called me at the fire station that morning, hoping to make plans. I'd told him we'd need to play it by ear because I might be too tired.

And the fact was—I *was* too tired.

Too tired of everything.

I stripped off, got under the covers, and pointed my remote at the TV.

Just before I pushed the power button, an image came into my head. That guy from Sidetrack last winter— the guy with the big mustache and the terminal case of shyness.

I don't know why he came to me in that moment. I mean, yes, he was cute. And his fear and vulnerability brought out something protective in me. But I'd seen countless men since last winter, both from a distance and, from time to time, more up close and personal.

Why was this one man stuck in my head? Was it simply because he was unexplored and, thus, free from defect?

I threw the remote control on my nightstand, deciding I was too tired for even TV. Besides, I thought it might be kind of nice drifting off to sleep with an image of *him* in my brain.

I turned over and closed my eyes, feeling a phantom arm reach around me to draw me close. That's all I've ever wanted.

I'm a simple man with simple needs.

Chapter Eight

RANDY

It was time to emerge from my hole again.

Hole, I suppose, is too crude and too mean to describe my home with my wife and son. I love them both with all my heart and our time together is sweet, surprisingly without much conflict or strife.

If only...

After the debacle of trying to go out last winter and ending up in that café, where I felt like someone who simply didn't belong in the gay world—whatever *that* was—I hid.

For months. And, for a while, our family evenings at home began to seem like normal like my attempted suicide in the hotel had never happened. I could forget. I could tell myself, *maybe I can just go on this way... It'll be easy. Just play the part.*

And then I would see the line of thinking as the betrayal it was—to who I am deep down. To my soul. To my well-being. To my sanity.

I'd read somewhere something along the lines of: once you wear a mask too long, you can't remove it without tearing away some of your skin.

It was an odd place I was in. I knew I was gay and thought I was coming to terms with that fact. Yet, acting on my attractions seemed too hard, too much to handle (and neither of those things in a good way).

And I thought even if I did act on my feelings or make a move toward that end, I'd just find I didn't belong in the gay world either.

That was my big fear—that I didn't belong anywhere.

This is where my therapist, Marshall, came into the picture. After I'd confessed my paralysis toward exploring my sexuality a little more fully (and that could be defined simply as finally having a gay friend or two—someone who might understand me, accept me for just who I was, rather than who I thought I was supposed to be) to Violet, she suggested I find someone to talk to.

"I can talk to you, can't I?" I'd asked her, playing dumb.

She patted my thigh. "Yes, always. But maybe it's time to, as Ann Landers so often put it, 'seek professional help.'"

"But we can't afford that."

Violet had looked at me like I was crazy. And maybe I was. Maybe I am.

A flicker of pain crossed her features—I could see it in her eyes, the way she held her lips. She pushed back some of her hair from her forehead and shook her head, eyeing me with disdain. "We can't afford for you *not* to go. You should have already been going." She looked down at the floor. "I don't want to find you dead in some hotel room. I don't want to have to explain something like that to Henry. He deserves better. *You* deserve better."

And what about you, my dear?

Yet I knew Violet was right. I'd known since before I'd tried to kill myself (just stating those words caused a pain more horrible in my gut than anything physical could cause).

Marshall Hissom had an ad in the back of the *Windy City Times* newspaper. He specialized in treating gay men. Bingo.

I'd seen him once a week throughout the winter. He was a kind, older man, with round gold-rimmed glasses, unruly gray hair contrasted with a very neat, closely trimmed beard. He favored corduroy, flannel, and fleece. His office, all warm cherrywood and leather, seemed like a sanctuary to me from the very first visit. The soft lighting and utter stillness made Marshall's office like a place I wanted to curl up and go to sleep.

I don't want to go into all the things we talked about, much of it, I suppose, your standard self-loathing gay man fare—how my father never loved me, my mother was too overbearing, even if she was well meaning, how I was bullied by other boys growing up—but the core of what we got to in our sessions was one simple fact.

I was okay.

I was a good man.

That may seem like nothing if you're reading this and never thought of yourself as different, an outsider. If you grew up feeling like you were normal, just one of the gang. Popular. Loved for who you were—and secure in that knowledge.

Knowing I was okay was a revelation. Not just okay, but capable of being loved and accepted. See, *before* I wore my mask so fulltime that I felt like it was welded onto my face. I thought if anyone knew what was under there, they'd hate me, shirk me, want me as far away from them as possible.

The worst part of that feeling was that *I* agreed with it. I understood it.

In the contest of who hated me most, I came up a clear winner.

For so long, I didn't want to be *me*. That sounds absurd, but it was true.

Marshall showed me that I was a good person. Hating myself was only destroying me.

"Do you believe in God, Randy?" he asked during one of our sessions.

I had to think about it. I'd been brought up Catholic, baptized and confirmed. In my darkest moments, I felt that a lot of the shame and guilt I felt about who I was came from the Church. Their hypocrisy was what drove me away—even though to this day, I treasure the rituals and simple beauty of Mass.

But I don't think Marshall was trying to get at my religious upbringing here. I had a sense he had an overarching point he wanted to make.

"Yeah, sure. As an old man in the sky, casting judgment down? No. But I do believe there's something out there that unites us all, that makes us all one."

Marshall nodded, his hand on his chin. "So this *something*. Do you think it's perfect?"

"It's God."

"That's not what I asked."

"Well, yeah. As the energy that manifests the universe, I would say that yes, he or she or it must be perfect. A divine ideal we can strive for."

"If God is perfect, then it must also follow that he—or she or it—doesn't make mistakes, no?"

I nodded, although I was getting a headache trying to sort out which mistakes I'd seen throughout my life were man-made or God-made.

He caught my eye. "You're not a mistake." He let out a little sigh. "So, stop telling yourself you are. You don't need to be anything other than the very best version of you that you can."

It was good that those words ended that particular session because it gave me a lot to think about.

Marshall also showed me I needed to leave my marriage, to get out and experience the life I paradoxically dreamed of and dreaded. And he thought I should make the break sooner rather than later.

This latter notion we were still exploring, the logistics, how it would affect all of us. I wasn't ready to move in that direction...not yet, not quite.

He brought me to the point where I found myself this unseasonably warm evening in late April.

I'm poised and ready to head out the front door...

Yet my thoughts are not anticipatory. They're about what I'm leaving, not just tonight, but most likely, eventually, for good. I feel like the pushmi-pullyu creature from Dr. Doolittle.

I was finishing up getting ready in the bathroom when Violet knocked on the door. "Can I come in?" she called from the hallway.

"Sure." I'd just finished brushing and flossing and was now getting ready to shave. I stood before the medicine cabinet mirror in my underwear—a pair of white Fruit-of-the-Loom briefs. I wore a beard of shaving cream and had the basin filled with steaming water. I knew that one day, maybe in the not too distant future, I'd miss this easy familiarity.

Violet slipped in and sat on the closed toilet seat. She had a glass in her hand.

"What's that?" I gestured toward the glass with my shaver.

"Vodka and tonic."

"No lime?"

She shook her head. "We don't have any. I put an extra shot in to make up for the loss of the lime."

I noticed that Violet had been drinking more lately, and I wished it wasn't so, longing to rest comfortably in the knowledge that her alcohol consumption was *not* because of me. I just hoped she had a handle on things.

"I just got Henry down for the night and thought I'd have this." She raised her glass, shaking it so the ice rattled. "To help me unwind."

I nodded and began shaving my neck with upward strokes. Throughout the winter, I'd had a full beard. I'd only recently shaved it off. I had Henry stand on the toilet seat, watching his daddy's transformation so it wouldn't come as a shock to him.

I left the mustache.

Marshall said that my shaving off the beard was symbolic—a way of letting my true "face" emerge. I don't know about that.

Sometimes a shave is just a shave.

"Where are you off to tonight?" Violet asked. She was bracing herself for a reply even if she already knew the answer. Marshall was right. I did need to get out of our shared apartment. I couldn't help but feel guilty about leaving her and Henry alone even if she did encourage me. "You should be out there meeting people like yourself. Making some friends. Really, everything will fall into place. But that can't happen if you're at home with Henry and me, watching *Cheers*."

The problem was I didn't know if any "people like myself" existed.

I told her, "I thought I'd head back down to Halsted. There's a bar called North End down there, a few blocks from Wrigley Field. I hear it's kind of low-key."

"What does that even mean?"

I pondered how to phrase my answer. "Well, to me, it means it's not a pickup spot."

"Not cruisy?"

I laughed. "Where did you pick up the word cruisy?" In my role as a straight man, I'd never heard anything, even a singles bar, described as cruisy.

"I read." She sipped her drink. "Why does it always have to be a bar?"

I rinsed my face and then drained the sink. "What do you mean?"

"Why do you always have to go out to gay *bars*? You've never been a big drinker. And, if I wanted to meet a man, I wouldn't necessarily go to a bar. Most of 'em are meat markets, Randy."

I didn't tell her I'd recently heard of a gay bar that actually had meat market in its name. I didn't even want to think about what went on in such a place. It both terrified and tantalized me.

I toweled off my face and examined it in the mirror. The person looking back at me was someone I felt was new, someone I was just beginning to know. I smiled and then turned away, feeling foolish.

"I know, but number one—I'm not going out to *meet men*. I'm just hoping to find maybe a kindred spirit out there: someone who at least understands, on a personal level, what I'm going through. Maybe someone who can help me better see how this all works. It's a whole new world." I was fudging on the truth, I know, a little. There was a part of me that *did* want to meet men, or a man, but admitting that to Violet was impossible at this stage.

I could barely admit it to myself. My baser desires had yet to break free of my dreams, or at least my fantasies when my guard was most down.

"And number two," I began, moving from the bathroom to the bedroom. I motioned her to follow me and she did. "Number two—" I continued, searching through my closet for a nice shirt to pair with my jeans. "—I don't know any other way to meet gay people." That statement, too, was *not* the whole truth and nothing but the truth. I'd seen advertisements in the gay papers for all sorts of clubs, groups, and sports teams. But a bar was just easier. I could hide in a bar if I wanted to. If I went, for example, to the gay euchre club that met every Tuesday night at a bar (again, with the bars!) on Sheridan, I'd be forced to talk, to be "out" in a way I didn't know if I was comfortable with yet.

"Really?" Violet nudged me aside and pulled a brown-and-yellow flannel shirt from my closet and handed it to me. "Wear this. It brings out the brown in your eyes." She smiled, but it was tight-lipped and didn't reach her own eyes.

"Thanks." I took the shirt from her and wondered if I'd have the courage to admit to anyone I might meet later tonight that my wife had picked out the shirt I wore.

After I was dressed, Violet looked at me with sadness in her blue eyes. "You have fun tonight," she said quickly and, even more quickly, turned and left the room. I heard her pouring another drink for herself. And then I heard the theme music from *Cheers*.

It seemed ironic. A place where everybody would know my name...

And now I find myself on the L platform at Jarvis, just a block away from our little two-bedroom apartment on Fargo Avenue.

It's unseasonably warm for April, and I wonder if the flannel was a mistake. I could always just take the shirt off and go bare-chested. I'm sure there were bars where I wouldn't be out of place...

I'll be fine.

The train squeals into the station and I board. I sit near the front and am glad the car's half empty—or half full depending on whether I'm being optimistic. I settle in and stare out the window, watching the backs of brick apartment buildings go by, trying to catch a glimpse into the lives revealed by their lighted windows. There's a guy in his kitchen, standing at a stove, wearing nothing but pink bikini briefs. A couple sits on a couch, their faces barely lit by the flickering blue illumination of a TV. A dog appears to be barking on the back porch landing of one of the buildings as we go by.

When we get to the station at Wilson, a young guy gets on. He has frizzy dark hair, a stubbly face, and odd, too-pale blue eyes. There's something crazy about those eyes, which he immediately focuses on me.

I stare back out the window, trying to ignore him, but I can feel the laser intensity of his gaze. It actually makes the hair on the back of my neck rise.

I glance back at him, and he's got a sort of half grin on his face. He looks dirty and disheveled, but there's something about him that's also weirdly sexy—in a dangerous way. Like, you know, in the way Ted Bundy was sexy. Like me, he's wearing jeans and a flannel shirt, but his jeans are faded to almost white and ripped in several places. His shirt, a plaid pattern of cream, blue, and black, is wrinkled and looks like it should have been thrown in the wash a long time ago—or maybe even the rag bag. There's a dark brown stain near the unraveling edge at the bottom of the shirt. I force myself to think this is *not* a blood stain.

Once he knows I'm looking, he intensifies his stare. I feel as though our gazes are locked. Even if I want to, I can't look away. I think of the old Dracula movies I watched as a kid.

Why's he looking at me, anyway? I'm just one of many commuters on the train.

And then I know. He licks his lips and lets a hand whisper across his crotch.

Oh my God, he's cruising me. I know it intuitively. And no, kids, this is not me flattering myself. I didn't ask for his attention, nor do I want it.

How does he even know I'm gay?

Or is he just playing the odds? It shouldn't bother me. The guy is yet another weirdo stranger on the CTA, which hardly makes him unique, but I'm bothered that he sees something in me that must make him think his flirting, if you can call it that—it seems a lot more sinister—is welcome.

I get up and move to the rear of the train and then pass through the doors connecting the cars, which I know I'm not supposed to do.

Thankfully, he doesn't follow. I stand, as he did, in the next car, waiting for the stop at Addison to come up.

It bugs me that maybe I'm not as hidden as I thought—that maybe I'm not as "straight acting and appearing" as they say in the ads at the back of the gay rags. Does the whole world know, from just a look, that I'm a big old 'mo? Am I simply deluding myself thinking it's not as plain as the nose on my face—or the bulge in the crotch of my jeans?

Perhaps coming out won't be as arduous a process as I feared. Maybe *I'm*, really, the last to know?

Why does it bug me, anyway? I've come to the point where I know I *am* gay, so why should it matter if someone can tell from looking at me? Is that so horrible?

Don't answer that.

HOURS LATER, I find myself hugging the same bit of wall I started out with at the beginning of the night here at North End. I've had a couple of beers and watched people come and go. Why does everyone seem so comfortable? Why does it feel like I'm the only one who's out of place? And, maybe most importantly, will I never shake this feeling of being an outsider, the one loner who doesn't belong?

I glance around the bar once again. It's a fairly good-sized joint, and all I see are smiling, laughing faces. Guys drinking. Guys playing pool. Guys flirting. They all seem as though they're born to this lifestyle.

Strike that. In my head, Marshall reminds me, *you do not have a lifestyle. You have a life. And what you make of that life is up to you.*

What I feel like making of my life right now is to run and hide again in the security and safety of my home. I thought my wife and even my child were the only things that were holding me back.

But maybe they're my sanctuary, my burrow that I scurry into.

Maybe, I'm finally catching on, the only thing holding me back is me. No one's really stopping me from living the life I want, I need...hell...I was *born* to live. Not even a female wife.

"You should smile." A voice reaches me, coming from my side.

I turn to look and there's no one there...well, at least, until I direct my gaze downward a bit.

A guy in a wheelchair has rolled up next to me. He's a good bit older, with a bald pate and salt-and-pepper, close-cropped hair around his temples. Unlike most of the guys in the bar, who favor the jeans and T-shirt uniforms, he's wearing a pressed Oxford button-down shirt, khakis, and tassel loafers. He looks like he just stepped out of an LL Bean catalog.

Before I saw he was handicapped, I was about to snap something back at him along the lines of telling him to mind his own business, which was wrong, handicapped or not. But the fact that he's different from everyone else in the bar makes me temper my grouchiness. And maybe that's a good lesson to learn across the board.

"Why's that?" I ask and give him a smile.

"Aw, see there." He points to my face. "That's why. You've got a beautiful smile! It lights up your face. Why hide it?" His voice is gravelly. "I've been watching you and, honestly, buddy, you look scared out of your wits."

"I do?"

"Come on." He rolls his eyes and then takes a sip from the short glass he holds in his left hand. Bourbon or Scotch swirl around in the glass, catching the light, going dark. "You don't *look* dumb, although that's no guarantee you're not. I say that not to flatter you, but because I think you're self-aware enough to know your frown telescopes your fear and discomfort at being here—in a bar filled with queers." He giggles, which doesn't match the sandpapery quality of his speaking voice.

"Queers?" I'm shocked.

"It's what we are, right? All the cool kids have appropriated the term, rendering it, ostensibly, harmless.

I don't know about that, but I'm on board with the intention."

I laugh and shake my head. "You're funny."

"But then looks aren't everything, right?" He finishes his drink.

"No! No. That's not what I meant at all."

"Oh, don't be oversensitive. You'll have to work harder to offend me. And believe me, I've had my share of jokers who think they can insult me, but I've learned to just let it roll off my back and onto the motor of this contraption to which I've been unfortunately confined." He shakes his empty glass at me. "Buy me a drink?"

I take his empty glass. "Who *are* you?"

"Name's Stephen." He then adds, "Hawking," and cracks himself up.

"Am I going to regret this?" I hold up his empty glass. I already know I'll buy him that drink, because this guy has succeeded in doing the impossible—he's made me forget myself for a few minutes, and more importantly, he's made me laugh. I didn't think laughter was a possibility tonight.

"Probably. But while you have many so-called, able-bodied gents from which to choose this fine spring evening, none of them have my wit, charm, or intelligence."

"Not to mention modesty?"

"That too." He points to the glass. "That's Maker's Mark, from my home state of Kentucky. I take it neat, as any real Southern gentleman would."

I nod. "Right." I hurry to the bar and order another Miller Lite from the dark-bearded bartender and, of course, a Maker's Mark—a double. I feel curiously unburdened and am not quite sure I understand why.

The bartender sets the drinks down in front of me and takes my cash. When he offers me my change, I tell him to keep it, even though it's way more than twenty percent.

"Thanks, cutie," he says and winks. He adroitly sweeps the change off the bar and stuffs it into the pocket of his way-too-tight Levi 501s. I don't have the nerve to ask him if the bulge in them is real, or a sock—perhaps one of the ones that we can never seem to find a mate for after drying. As I pick up the glass and my bottle, he leans close and says, "Don't let Stephen take you for all your worth."

"Oh?"

"Yeah. He may be confined to a wheelchair, but he's nimble where it counts."

"Okay."

I walk back to Stephen and tell myself the bartender sounded good-natured in his warning. I shouldn't worry too much about my new friend.

Or should I?

"Thank you, kind sir." Stephen takes the glass from me. After a sip, he wipes his mouth with his hand. "Mother's milk."

I chuckle.

He points. "Got you to smile."

"You could probably get me to do a lot of things." Really, he could. There's something charming about him, yes, but I would take it a step further and say that another *c* word applies—charismatic.

"Oh really?" He wiggles his eyebrows a la Groucho Marx. "You're flirting with me, and you have me at a disadvantage. I don't even know your name."

"Randy."

"Is that your name? Or how you're feeling?"

"Can't it be both?"

"Of course. In which case, it's a very apt name indeed."

We drink and are quiet for a moment. But, as expected, Stephen pipes up first. "About the flirting—" he begins.

I wonder what I've gotten myself into.

"Yes?" I take a long swallow of beer and eye the door.

"Although you're a very charming fellow, with a pretty face and a bitching bod, flirting will get you nowhere with me."

"Oh? I thought you were hitting on me."

"Don't flatter yourself, dear boy. I was simply being friendly to someone I perceived might need a little attention. See, believe it or not, I know how being in a bar alone can feel awkward."

"You do? You seem so at ease."

"Enough with the flattery. I wasn't always so comfortable, and it isn't just because I'm in a wheelchair." He gives me a different kind of smile, one imbued with warmth. I see the kindness as a glimmer in his brown eyes, even behind the lenses of his tortoiseshell glasses. "Believe it or not, I'd bet just about every fella in here has been in your shoes at one time or another. Scared. Feeling out of place. Wondering—do I really belong here?" He smiles up at me, and it makes me feel singled out, but in a good way. "You're not as special as you think." And even those words, which could be construed as insulting, seem kind.

"I'm not, am I." It's not a question. All at once, I realize he's right. Everyone in here tonight probably had to take a few tentative steps into going out into the community at first. They, too, may have had no friends or support when they first came out—only the need to be with other people like them, even if they paradoxically believed these folks were nothing like them.

"We're all different," Stephen says and takes another sip. "And we're all alike. Like lamps."

"Lamps?"

"Are you a parrot?"

I draw myself up with indignation. "I am a mynah bird, sir. I'll thank you to remember the distinction."

That gets him to chuckle. "Lamps because we're all different. Some are table lamps, some desk, some floor, some night-lights...but we all have the same light inside of us."

"We're all looking for the same thing?"

"I didn't say that. But yeah, we all came here to step out of a world that might reject us, even hate us, and to step into a place where we know, even a little bit, we're seen and accepted for who we are. Safe. That's at the heart of why everyone's here. I think, anyway. And take my opinion, add a fiver, and you can buy yourself another beer."

We both laugh and quietly observe the crowd for a while.

"Are you married?" Stephen asks after a time.

"Is it that obvious?"

"As obvious as the *band on the third finger of your left hand*." That cracks him up. Before I can reply, he says, "Even if you'd slid that ring off and tucked it into your pocket, it would be obvious, darling. Now, you have the right clothes on. You're obsessively *neat*, but your fear sets you apart. I've been hanging out in bars long enough to spot a married man when I see one." He lowers his eyelids a bit. "There's something furtive about them. And they're not as rare as you might think."

"Yes. I'm married." There's no use in denying it. He's already seen my simple gold band. "Got a wife up in Rogers Park."

"Kids?"

I think of little Henry, on his back in his twin bed, slumbering, his thumb stuffed into his mouth, even though we're trying to get him to stop that before he goes into first grade. What will *he* think of his old man once he's old enough to understand? Will he shun me? The thought is almost enough to make me excuse myself from Stephen and head out into the warm spring night.

But all I've done, my whole life, is run away. Maybe it stops here. Tonight. "I have a little boy. His name's Henry."

"Henry. How old-fashioned. I would imagine you're feeling some guilt, along with the self-consciousness."

"You'd be right. Can we talk about something else?"

He ignores the question. "Do you have a picture?"

I debate. But in the end my pride as a dad wins out. I pull out my wallet and show him a snapshot I took of Henry last summer on Fargo beach. He's standing knee-deep in the freezing water of Lake Michigan, wearing shorts, a striped T-shirt, and a brave smile. His eyes are wide. His nose is sunburned, and his dark curly hair is caught in a breeze.

Stephen gently takes my wallet from my hands. He lifts his glasses up to his forehead to peer down at my son and smiles. He hands me back my wallet. "He's got your nose."

I grin, flattered.

"Poor kid."

The smile disappears.

I decide I have nothing to lose, so I tell him, "He's a big part of the reason why, at age thirty-two, I'm out in a gay bar for only the second time."

He nods. "When did you realize you were gay?"

I don't think. An image pops into my head. I'm in my bedroom back in East Liverpool, Ohio. The little two-bedroom house I grew up in faced one of the busier streets in town. It's summer, hot, and the curtains at my window hang still, drooping in the humidity. A box fan is in the window at the top of the stairs, rotating noisily, doing nothing more than displacing the ninety degree air.

It's tough to sleep.

On our busy street, boys hitchhike. They're out there at all hours of the day and night. And my twelve-year-old self likes to watch them. They're usually teenagers or maybe early twenties. Young, anyway. Bad boys who get in cars with strangers, heedless.

They make me feel weird, low in my gut. The feeling is both pleasurable and nauseating at the same time.

Tonight is no exception. Across the street is a blue-jeaned young man with shoulder-length, stringy blond hair. He's wearing an old, faded T-shirt with the sleeves cut off so much that one can see the smooth skin of not only his arms, but his sides, a bit of chest, a nipple when he moves the right way. The streetlight above gives his skin a yellowish cast. His cigarette glows in the dark.

I'm mesmerized.

Suddenly, the spell shatters.

Because of the fan, I haven't heard my father creep up the stairs. All at once, he's behind me and then squatting next to me. Smiling, he peers out the same window and asks, "What are you looking at?"

But there's no need to respond. The answer is obvious, out there in the dark, where the handsome bad boy stands in a pool of light, smoking and hoping for a ride.

My father's smile disappears. He takes me in, almost as if he's never seen me before. He looks outside once more, perhaps hoping that something else, something other than a sexy, dangerous boy, has caught my attention. But all is still out there—the same houses, the same cracked, water-stained retaining wall that keeps the tree-covered hill above our street from washing down into it.

Quietly, he stands up and then slips away. I hear the bathroom door, across from my room, close.

Heat burns my face, and I scurry back into bed, pulling the sweat-damped sheet up to my chin. I'm not alone in my twin bed. Shame, big and imposing, spoons with me.

My father knows.

A week after that, he suggests we swap bedrooms, my parents and me. That way, I'm at the back of the house, where my window will look on to our own backyard and that of our neighbor's.

"I probably knew when I was around twelve," I finally answer Stephen.

Stephen shakes his head. "So why wait twenty years to come out? Why get married?"

"Oh Stephen, don't you know? There's a huge difference between *knowing* something and *accepting* it."

Stephen thinks about that for a second, and then he nods. "Okay," he says quietly. "I get it."

We don't speak for a time. And it's not long before a guy approaches us. He's stunningly handsome, with the kind of Nordic good looks that remind me of Robert Redford, perhaps in *The Way We Were*. Or maybe a young Nick Nolte. His blue eyes are crystalline, like frozen water, and the lashes are too long for a man, but they frame his eyes so beautifully as to be hypnotic.

His body, in faded jeans, tight white T, and cowboy boots, is taut, lean, well-muscled.

He's one of my filthiest fantasies, come to swaggering, grinning life.

And he's approaching me! I nervously assemble my features into a smile and find myself unable to meet his gaze.

He stops and looks down at Stephen. I quickly realize the mistake I've made. "I was wondering where you were." He leans over to plant a quick peck on Stephen's lips, then straightens to smile at me. "I hope he's not being too annoying. I'm Rory." He extends his hand and I shake it.

"The old ball and chain," Stephen mumbles, but grins.

"This is your—" I stop, flabbergasted. What do people say these days? Lover? Boyfriend? Friend?

Stephen smirks. "Yes, this is my beloved. My one and only. My soul mate." He eyes me with mock menace and then jabs a finger hard enough into my ribs to make me gasp. "And don't look so damn surprised."

Rory smiles. "I'll have you know that I was the one doing the chasing in this relationship. And he wasn't easy to catch." They both laugh.

"I played hard to get for six long months, unheard of in the gay world." He eyes Rory and the love there is plain. "That was seven years ago. Best thing that ever happened to me."

I'm embarrassed because I'd made a horrible assumption—that this wheelchair-bound man and this hunk could have never been a couple. I'm ashamed of myself, and I hurt because I'm willing to bet other people draw the same conclusion that I have. Now that the prejudicial scales have fallen from my eyes, I can see Stephen and Rory for what they are—two men in love.

And, for maybe the first time, I see that as a beautiful thing: real, and not something to be hidden away in the shadows.

"I'd like to buy both of you guys a drink. How 'bout it?"

"Oh, this one here'd let you buy him drinks all night," Rory says. "But we need to get home. We have a shop to run, and weekends are our busiest time. We have to be up at the crack of dawn."

"Dawn is *not* a woman," Stephen adds. It takes me a second to catch on to the joke, and when I do, I roll my eyes. "But next time?"

"Sure." The bar doesn't seem like such a foreign place anymore. I'm excited that I've made my first friends even though I know I may never see them again.

"Will there *be* a next time?" I ask, betraying my lack of confidence.

Stephen cocks his head. "Of course, darling, aren't you having us over to meet the wife and kid?"

I go cold and realize that my skin has probably gone pure white.

"Joke. But Rory and I would love to invite *you* to dinner sometime. Maybe next week? Wouldn't we, Rory?"

Rory, whose focus has been on the TV screen where a Janet Jackson music video plays, looks back at Stephen. "Huh?"

"I was just telling Randy here that we'd like to have him over for dinner sometime. He's a carnivore, darling, so you can make him your *cabbonade*." He glances up at me. "You eat meat, right?"

"Like it's going out of style." I don't know what cabbonade is, but the prospect of being invited over for dinner sends a frisson of joy through me.

"Then, if you're free, maybe a night next week? We live up north a ways, on Marine Drive."

I nod. "I'd love to."

"Give him a card, Rory."

Rory gropes in the pocket of his tight-fitting jeans and pulls out a simple white card with black, raised lettering.

Stephen Link
Rory Fitzanko
(312) 555-9608

"Keep that in a safe place, and give us a call once you've had a chance to consult your calendar." He winks. "And your wife."

They start together toward the door. Stephen calls out, "Although I regret to say the invitation is only for you, darling. Only for you."

"Nice meeting you," I call out and watch them leave.

After a moment, I attempt to take a swig of beer and find my bottle is empty. I decide it's time to go home. Maybe I didn't get lucky tonight, but perhaps I found an even more important kind of intimacy—friendship.

And honestly, the prospect of getting lucky is still a scary thing. But I can't deny that it's becoming more and more tantalizing. And yet, I can't imagine a quick and casual sexual encounter. Most guys, straight or gay, seem to relish the prospect of such a thing. No strings. Just hot sex and then—see ya.

Not me. I'm cursed or blessed because I'm old-fashioned—a romantic. I lost my straight virginity with Violet. No, not on our wedding night, but we didn't do anything until we both knew we were in a committed relationship.

I want what Stephen and Rory appear to have. Right now, it seems like wishing I'll win the lottery, though. Between my own nervousness and discomfort with myself and the fast and loose playing field of gay bars, I'm beginning to see a relationship as some kind of holy grail.

I walk up to the bar and set my empty on it. I smile a good night at the bartender who winks at me. The wink makes me shiver a little deep down.

I shoulder my way through the crowd and head out into the night.

The air is a bit colder, but I'm warm enough in my flannel. Halsted is curiously quiet, and when I look up, I can actually make out a few stars. They're brave enough to shine, despite Chicago's light pollution, and I think there's a message in there for me somewhere, but my brain's too clouded by fatigue and beer to figure out what it is.

I head south, toward the Addison stop, even though Irving Park might be just a tiny bit closer. By going south, I'll pass more of my newfound brethren in their native habitat. Maybe a potential Prince Charming is also heading out of a bar, making his way to the L stop. Perhaps we'll eye each other shyly on the street, then hurry our separate ways. When we get to the L platform, we'll recognize each other and smile. At the last minute, one of us will rush to get on the same car with the other. As the car rocks its way north, we'll play a game of looking and then looking away, both electrified by the attraction ramping up between us. He's got a shaved head, gold wire-rim glasses, and a runner's body. He's clutching a dog-eared and broken spine copy of James Joyce's *Ulysses*. He rises to leave the train at Morse, which is only one stop before my own. I get up and follow, unsure of what my next move will be but thinking I could ask him about the book. Maybe I could tell him I tried to read it as an English major in college, but it all sailed over my head, making me yearn for the literary comfort food of someone like Stephen King.

I shake the fantasy from my head, fearing it's too sweet of a story to ever come true.

As I walk slowly, I consider practicing the swiveling head flirting I'm beginning to notice. I see it more and more now, and, sometimes, it's even directed at me, which makes the fire rise to my cheeks. I think about getting home too. Creeping into Henry's room and just watching him sleep—few pleasures are more sublime.

And then something new captures my interest. I hear voices, raised in argument, as I near a dark bowling alley parking lot.

"You used me and tossed me away like a fuck rag."

A line like that does cause one to perk up one's ears, doesn't it? I mean, you just don't hear it on the *Golden Girls* even if Blanche might say it. The voice saying the line is screechy, a little high, teetering on the edge of hysteria. There's also a crazy kind of threatening surliness to it that reminds me of Martha in *Who's Afraid of Virginia Woolf?*

I step under the shadow of a store awning and peer around the corner to find the source of the voice.

Caught between the hulking silhouettes of parked cars and a graffiti-laden brick wall are two men. I can't really make out much detail, but they're both of the burly variety, broad in the beams as my grandma would say. Bears, as I'm learning to call them.

The other guy answers and sounds more reasonable. "Dude! Calm down."

I wonder if anyone in the history of the world has ever calmed down when being told to.

"Fuck you!" The other guy screams back, proving my point. I have to wonder if this encounter will come to blows, and not the kind most people think of as occurring in the dark shadows of Halsted Street byways.

"Listen. I'm sorry, okay? You're right. I could have handled things better. I should have called you. We should have talked. That's on me. I was a coward. I've been mad myself at guys who suddenly up and stop calling, avoiding me. It pisses me off, and I think it shows a lack of character. And then I go and do the same damn thing. Shame on me, seriously. But, Dean, listen, I don't have an excuse. And I don't expect you to forgive me. But I do want you to know I apologize. I regret not being more open. Hurting your feelings. You deserve better."

There's quiet for a while. Then the other guy, Dean I guess, speaks in a kind of soft, wheedling tone. I can barely make out what he's saying, but I hear enough to know that he's pathetically asking if maybe they could have just one more chance.

Oh man, have some dignity.

The quiet stretches out, almost like a fog floating forward from the back of the parking lot.

Then the first guy, the one being screamed at, says, "Dean. You're a nice guy and we had fun, but there was just nothing there."

"Nothing? Nothing? Nothing was good enough to screw me on your bed and in the hallway up to your apartment? Nothing was enough to let me blow you multiple times in public! Nothing is the promises you made about spending the summer together." Martha is back, full force.

I know I shouldn't be hearing this. But like someone passing a car accident on the side of the road, I simply can't look away. Or turn my ears away. Whatever.

I think our more reasonable member of this pair has given up. And I can't blame him. Dean has proven himself to be the kind of "victim" for whom no amount of arguing or apologizing will suffice.

All of a sudden, he's walking toward me, his heels clicking on the pavement. I lean in, hoping to vanish into the plate glass window of the storefront behind me. But the guy sees me, and when he does, he stops and regards me.

"I know you," he says. A faltering smile whispers across his features.

And he does look familiar, but at the moment, I'm too keyed up to recall where I might have seen him before.

"I don't think so," I mumble and begin to hurry away.

We most likely are confused, both of us. Chicago's a city of millions—how many lookalikes are out there? Plus, I hardly know anyone down in these parts, so the odds of recognizing him are slim.

"Yeah!"

I start to move away.

Dean catches up and shoves the familiar-looking guy out of the way as he heads for the street. He catches sight of me and narrows his eyes. "Get an earful?" He heads away from us. "Keep away from this jerk. He's a user."

I don't say anything. Dean walks off into the night, the flaps of his open flannel shirt trailing behind him. Was he wearing a harness?

"We met before," the other guy says when Dean's out of earshot. "I remember."

I look at him. He's cute. Sexy in a tough, yet cuddly way, like the bear I suppose he is. Black, curly hair. Impish grin. His ears stick out a little too far, yet somehow manage to be alluring rather than comical.

He's eyeing me, waiting, presumably, for me to speak up, to say where we've run into each other.

But I draw a blank.

And the spat I witnessed has put me off. I want to scurry back to the safety of my warren in Rogers Park. "I don't know about that. I need to get on my way, though. Have a good night."

I don't look back at him as I hurry south. But I can feel his gaze on me, watching, watching...

Chapter Nine

JOHN

What was his name? I couldn't forget that face—ever. But his name? It's just there, right out of reach.

He heads south on Halsted. As I watch him, I get distracted by the fact that he looks just as good walking away as he does from the front. Is he an old trick? Someone I brought home from Little Jim's one lonely night? Did we meet on that cursed phone sex line and I went over to his place? Did he once date my best friend, Vince? *That's* a possibility. Vince has had a go-round with about every gay and questioning male this side of fifty in the Chicagoland area. Choosy, he's not.

But none of these scenarios match. There's a kind of mental alarm that goes off when you get something just right.

I know him. I want to know him. I knew him. The memory just will not surface. Here I am, still young, and already losing it.

I don't move until he's out of sight. A gaggle of early twentysomethings, laughing and hitting one another playfully, block his passage from my view. And when they clear, he's no more.

Maybe he was never there. Or maybe he moves in and out of reality, the gay male version of *Brigadoon*.

Maybe he's the elusive *one* I've searched for all my adult life, rare and fantastic as a unicorn.

I breathe in the night air, inhaling deeply and letting it out slowly, as I turn and head up the street toward North End.

My nerves are still jangling from my encounter with Dean. I'm not used to conflict, to being put on the spot, to being challenged. He reminds me of Glenn Close in *Fatal Attraction*. He's got that same kind of delusional, clinging mindset. They say hell hath no fury like a woman scorned. Whoever coined that little chestnut never met a jilted gay man. I should laugh, but it's not funny.

Dean didn't stop calling, not back when he tore up my number live on my answering machine and then mercifully said I'd never hear from him again. But now, the coward doesn't have the nerve to say anything when he dials me. He blocks his own number and calls and hangs up, over and over, at all hours. I can't think how many dreams he's interrupted.

I found the air let out of one of my tires one morning. Maybe him? Who knows? I don't want to be paranoid, but I also don't want to be cavalier about this guy, who's obviously nuts.

Like tonight, I suspect he was lying in wait for me in the bowling alley parking lot where I often chance parking, even though I'd pay out the ass if I was ever caught and towed by the Lincoln Park Pirates. I have no idea how he'd know where I'd be, other than my telling him at one point about my little parking secret, but I'm getting more and more the feeling he's following me—I catch little glimmers of someone out of the corner of my eye when I'm out and about, and I think it's him.

Maybe I'm the one who's nuts.

Or maybe I'm the one who'll end up stabbed in a back alley off of Halsted.

Yikes, John! Get your mind off the melodrama! Your life isn't a horror movie. Get busy and have some fun.

I'm at the entrance to North End. I lean against the wall, my shoulders resting against the cold brick. *Do I really want to go in?* Earlier, alone in my apartment, it had seemed like such a good idea. I had played The Go-Go's, an old fave, at top volume, as I danced around my apartment, getting dressed. I'd asked Vince to join me, but he's been seeing this dentist guy named Arvin up in Edgewater, and, wonder of wonders, the two of them have hit it off. He's staying in with Arvin tonight so they can try out Arvin's new laser disc player and watch old Russ Meyer movies.

Fun.

But the encounter with Dean has left me shaken. Shaky. I know alcohol might mute the jangle of my nerves, but I also think alcohol might dim and blur my memory.

And I want to remember where I saw that cute guy before.

I turn and open the door, peer inside for a minute. The bouncer has his hand out for my ID and eyes me questioningly.

After a moment, he asks, "You comin' in or not?"

I listen to my heart and say, "Not." I step aside to let a couple of guys, who smell of bourbon and cigarettes, slide in past me.

The street is once again quiet. It's not all that late, but I guess everyone's in their favorite watering hole by now, doing the mating dance of glances, awkward smiles, and more obvious signals like the cupping of a crotch. Lord help me.

I recall the crowd inside North End. They looked lively, happy. The music was loud, the chatter louder. Smoky air. Techno music. The crack of an eight ball hitting its target.

Normally, I'd want to dive right in that fine water of available men. Browse for a while and then pick one out that I could take home for the night—or he me. Maybe I would have ended up with the guy I met a few weeks ago, or someone like him, who lived in Lake Point Tower in one of the penthouses. More of a thrill than the tepid blow job he gave me was the view from the floor-to-ceiling windows—the black ink stain of Lake Michigan, the rising, gilded towers of the Chicago skyline, the long concrete peninsula of Navy Pier.

It was all magical until I woke to a gray dawn and tiptoed around, gathering up my clothes so I could sneak out. The man on the bed was snoring, a line of drool dribbling from the side of his mouth. In the wan light, he appeared decades older than he did to me the night before when soft lights, denial, and hard alcohol had imbued him with a kind of youthful exuberance. Now, he's just a scruffy older man, maybe even old enough to be my dad, with a pot belly and pitted scars on his face from teenage acne.

As I leave, he stirs a bit and mumbles, "Call me."

I thought, "I sure will." *Not.*

I'm thinking I'm already here, in Boystown, so why not see what the night, and the bars, have on offer? If I don't want to go to North End, there are other choices: dance clubs, leather bars, low-key hardcore drinking establishments, backroom bars with hardcore porn on the screens, even the bathhouse farther south.

That last place has come in handy when in need of a quick man fix. Yet, when I've walked its dim hallways and "play" rooms, I've always had this feeling of aloneness—there's a smell of desperation in the air, along with the bleach. All of this underscored by the techno beat of nameless, tuneless, house music. I've always looked around guiltily as I left, praying no one who knows me will be walking or driving by to see me emerge.

I could go to Roscoe's, maybe even see if I could engage my happy hips again. I've never been shy about dancing and have no fear of getting on the dance floor by myself if I have to. There's a certain appeal to just disappearing into some good, endless thumping music, closing my eyes, letting my body take over.

But not tonight. Tonight, I simply feel my movements would be awkward, stiff.

I could go to Sidetrack.

And when I think of Sidetrack, I remember. *That's where I saw the cute guy with the mustache. It was last winter. I tried to buy him a beer, but he was so scared you'd think I was Michael Myers brandishing a knife instead of a Budweiser.*

I wonder if that's where he was going tonight. Maybe I could try again.

Really, John? I don't know if he'd be happy to see you. Delight wasn't written across his face when you passed him. He denied remembering you, and even if that was true, he probably didn't get a very good impression of you or the company you keep after witnessing your altercation with Dean.

I shrug. I don't know if it was running into Dean or what, but the enthusiasm I had earlier for going out has vanished.

I get moving, heading east. I'll walk down by the lakefront, stare out at the water.

Maybe on the way, I'll see *him*.

OF COURSE, I don't see *him*. That kind of meetup only works in romantic comedies, when the two star-crossed lovers run into each other as part of some mix-up: say one of their dogs, slick with suds and bathwater, has escaped and is dashing headlong down a dark street, and the other scoops it up and hands it back to him.

I finally come to where the city ends. I've traveled a little south and ended up at the notorious Belmont Rocks, what passes for a gay beach in Chicago. In summer, the large graffiti-tagged boulders are home to legions of sunbathers, some wearing Speedos, others cutoff denim shorts, and still others, nothing at all. The "Rocks" is a party spot, a meeting destination, and a state of mind, especially in the late part of summer, when Lake Michigan gets warm enough to dip into without risking a coronary, and the summer sun heats libidos up enough to send them out in search of sustenance.

Tonight, the Rocks are empty. As if to underscore the loneliness of the scene, here in the midst of this crowded metropolis, a moaning wind, cold, moves across the lake to lift my hair and to cause my eyes to water.

I stroll through the darkness, feeling a kind of peace in this solitude.

And then I hear it, from somewhere below, near the crash and spray of the water as it slams into the boulders.

Someone weeping.

My first impulse makes me feel guilty. It's to quietly turn tail and head back west on Belmont toward the traffic and the bright lights. I rationalize this selfish notion by telling myself that whoever's down there on slippery rocks, crying, wants to be alone. He's gone to great pains to find a spot away from the rush, the hustle and bustle of the Lakeview neighborhood.

But I know that's not true. I just don't know if I'm up to comforting someone else when suddenly I feel so in need of it myself.

I make a soft *tsk* to myself, shaking my head. One thing I've learned is that we can heal ourselves not by reaching *in* but by reaching *out*. The fact that there's a fellow human being in pain near me should be cause to investigate, to see how I might help.

It's what I'd want someone to do for me.

I sit on the rocks and shimmy downward toward the cold and crashing waves.

I recognize him as soon as I get close. Recognition makes me wish I'd listened to my baser instincts.

He looks over at me, sniffs, and says, "You." It's not a statement of recognition but one of accusation.

I sidle across the surface of the boulder he's on so I can sit beside him. We eye each other. He sniffs again and wipes his nose on the sleeve of his flannel shirt. Sighing, he picks a pebble up and flings it into the water.

"Dean, I'm sorry...again. That things didn't work out between us." *Why am I doing this? We barely spent any time together. He's overreacting. We all get dumped.* "I should have been more honest with you, but I can't go back and undo it now."

I feel the burn of his stare through the darkness. At last, he says, "You don't even know."

"Know what?" I'm already thinking about my bed at home, and not in a sexual way, but sinking into the comfort of Mom's homemade quilt, flannel sheets, and my mound of feather pillows.

Dean's voice is soft, barely audible above the wind and the crash of the surf. "You think it's all about you. About us. When there was never really an us to begin with."

Who is this person, I wonder? I want to look again to check to make sure it is indeed Dean next to me.

"What? I'm sorry, dude, but you've been stalking me since we broke up. And I don't even know if broke up is right because we only went on a couple dates."

Dean sighs. He takes my hand in his, and my first impulse is to snatch it away, but I resist. I look over at him and my eyes have adjusted more fully to the dark. I hone in on something in his eyes I can't quite put my finger on. Is it caring? Resignation? Despair?

"I wasn't crying about *you*. I've shed all my tears over you." He lets loose a little laugh. "I realized after I came at you earlier tonight that, one, I was losing my dignity and not liking myself much; and two, what I thought I was in love with wasn't *you* at all, but an ideal, an image of you I made up from some truth and a lot of hope. Yeah, you're a cool, manly guy, very butch. Hot. Some might say a catch. But I wanted someone who was as into me as I was into him. And that wasn't you. That's not your fault. Hell, it isn't even personal."

"Okay," I say, unsure where this is headed.

"I got some news today."

The sentence hangs in the chill and damp of the night air. Like "We need to talk," the phrase he just uttered is seldom followed by anything good.

The nurturing side of me kicks in, even if it is Dean. "Everything okay?"

"No, John. Everything is *not* okay."

I turn a little more toward him. "What is it?"

I'm gay. I work as a paramedic, so I'm in the healthcare industry. I help people. I save people. I'm attuned to the news, both in papers and on TV, as well as the news that flows on the streets, especially in a gay ghetto like Boystown. I brace myself for what I suspect's coming.

No surprise here. No shocking twist.

"I went to my doc's today." He stops and I can hear him trying to tame his breathing. I don't say anything. I listen.

"It was, uh, just the usual checkup I have once a year, like getting my teeth cleaned."

"Uh-huh."

"And, uh, he said one of my tests came back with an *abnormal* result. Can you believe that? Abnormal? Please."

"Are you okay?"

"I guess. For now. You know what I'm talking about, don't you?"

I nod even though I hope, in an absurd way, that he's got lung cancer from all the smoking he does. Lung cancer, at least, is somewhat treatable. "I think I do, but why don't you tell me anyway?"

"I'm HIV positive."

Even though I suspected this was the crux, I'm taken aback. I suck in a breath.

Not many get out alive once they go inside the HIV funhouse.

"I'm sorry," I say and I mean it. I'm also rapidly and selfishly recounting my sex with him and wondering if I was ever a little less than careful.

I think I'm okay. Maybe.

But right now I have in front of me a person who is *not* okay and who's in need of comfort.

"They're coming up with new treatments all the time." I feel like I'm lying as I say this. The gay newspapers' obituary sections are full, every week, of pictures of young, smiling men who should be looking forward to decades more.

"Yeah, that's what they told me."

We're silent for a long time. Words and phrases rise to my consciousness, and they all seem banal, meaningless, superficial in light of life and death. So I simply repeat, "I'm sorry."

"I am too. For the longest time, I wondered if I was immune because I haven't exactly been Mary Poppins." He nudged me. "You know that."

I stay quiet, and a quick image comes to me: him in the dark backroom of a bar, on his knees on the gritty floor, milking loads out of strangers. I shudder and vow never to go back to those backrooms. Who knows what's being passed around in the name of pleasure?

"In a way, I'm kind of relieved. For the longest time, I worried. Worried at every little thing that came along. Is this bruise KS? Are these sniffles a sign of pneumonia? Is the sweaty pillowcase from a nightmare? Or from the virus getting its hooks in me and these are the dreaded night sweats?" He smiles. "I don't have to wonder anymore, and at least that fear's been lifted."

I nod. "I get it."

Even though I know I might regret it, I can't help but ask, "You wanna go back up? Get a cup of coffee? Piece of pie?"

He's still holding my hand and he squeezes it. "It wasn't wishful thinking."

"What?" I grin.

"You really are a sweetheart. A good guy. I'm the one who owes you an apology for being a spoiled brat when things didn't go my way."

"No worries."

"Yes, worries."

"Okay, okay, we're both sorry." I stand up and tug at his hand, but he doesn't rise. "Come on, let's get out of the cold. If you don't want coffee, I'll buy you a beer."

He looks up at me, a sad smile on his bearded face. "I'm okay here."

"Really? Come on, Dean. It's cold. And weird people come out down here at night. Besides you, I mean. You shouldn't be alone."

"John. You don't need to mother me. The one I have back in Fort Worth is plenty, let me tell you." He laughs. "I'll be okay. I just want to sit here and think. Think about what to do next. Who to tell. That kind of thing. I'll be fine."

"Are you sure?" I don't want to leave him here.

"I couldn't be surer. The doc said this isn't always a death sentence. That some people go on just fine for a long time. I have no symptoms. I haven't been sick. Who knows? Maybe I'm just a carrier."

That makes me shiver even more than the cold wind off the lake.

"Okay." I move away with reluctance. "You have my number?" I snap my fingers. "Oh, that's right. You tore it up."

He chuckles. "That was for show. It was my ComEd bill that I used for the sound effect. I still have your number."

"So, you'll call me in the morning?"

"Like, for a date?"

Before I can respond, he points to me and laughs. "Kidding. I know we're not gonna be a couple, especially not now." He stares out, watching the progress of a gray-tipped wave across black water. "But I will call, John. Maybe we can have breakfast."

"Sure," I say and begin to move away.

On second thought, I hurry back and kneel beside him. I take him in my arms and squeeze. "You're gonna be okay."

He clings to me. "I know. I am. I really am."

He lets go first, patting me on the back. "Now, give a girl some space."

I get up and begin the trek back to city lights.

1986, Summer

"The dreamy days and sticky nights of summer were already calling, as if anything could happen."
—C.J. Carlyon, The Cherry House

Chapter Ten

RANDY

It's miserable hot, the kind of heat that feels as though someone has thrown a wet blanket over you—one that's been soaked in boiling water. It presses down, a living thing, suffocating and uncomfortable.

The air is still. The leaves in the trees no longer whisper to one another; they're too tired. Even the snatches of music and conversation on the street are muffled as though humidity weighs them down. Everything seems to move in slow motion.

Chicago in August offers some of the worst weather in the country. When you consider that, with the worst winters in the US on the other end, you may wonder why anyone even lives here.

The extremes test the limits of human endurance.

Right now, the day is beginning to wind down; dusk waits in the wings. Our little walk-up on Fargo Avenue is not air-conditioned, so we have box fans placed in many of the windows, making lots of noise, but providing little in the way of relief. Hot, humid air blown around at a higher rate of speed is still hot, humid air. Still, it's better than nothing.

I'm out on our balcony overlooking the street below. Cars meander by, all headed west toward Paulina, because ours is a one-way street. It's Saturday night, so more traffic, more revelers, more L runs, more snatches of music—rock and hip-hop mostly—pouring from open car windows. A beat-up red Nissan Sentra is double-parked just west of our building. A man lays on the horn and cries out, "Raven! Hey Raven!"

There's a big maple in front of us. Its leaves hang lifelessly, nearly blocking the view of the white brick courtyard building across the street. The air feels almost viscous, mired in the heat and unrelenting humidity.

The only thing pretty about the night is the way the sky, when I lean forward and peer toward the west, has a kind of magic. Up top, it's already a deep navy, almost black, but as it makes its way down to the silhouettes of trees and buildings, layers appear. Below the navy is gray, then a dusty purple, and at last a brilliant band of tangerine, made all the more beautiful because I know its life span is only minutes. Night will chase it away soon.

I'm just out of the shower, wearing only a pair of camouflage cargo shorts.

Tonight will be different at our house, I think, stomach churning with a potent cocktail of dread and anticipation. Tonight marks the crossing of a line—and I wonder if we'll, any of us in our little family, ever be the same.

Over the spring, Violet and I have been working on things together—and apart. I sit with my therapist, Marshall, and voice my concerns about her and her survival after I leave. And I will leave; we both know this now. Half measures, like having an open relationship or inviting men into our bedroom to share, won't work. We both know doing something like either of those things will only cause us both pain.

Marshall appreciates my concern over Violet and tries, subtly, to reassure me that she will be okay. That just like I am, she's growing and trying to accept a new normal. And those things don't have to necessarily erase the love we feel for each other.

My thoughts are interrupted by Violet coming out to the balcony to join me. I smell a soft perfume, jasmine, before I turn to look at her.

And she's lovely. Wearing a pair of denim shorts and a pink-and-white striped V-neck T-shirt with sandals, she looks more like a young girl barely out of her teens than a long-suffering wife and mother.

At long last, a breeze rises up, almost as if to greet her, and lifts some of her honey-colored bangs off her forehead.

Something clutches inside me.

"Everything okay?" I ask.

She's taken Henry downstairs to our neighbor, Mrs. Roberts, who'll babysit tonight.

Violet smiles. "Oh, he barely noticed me leaving. She had *The Fox and the Hound* all queued up. Popcorn, with lots of butter, popped. Brownies cooling on the kitchen counter. And, the piece de resistance, she has AC! Henry won't want to come home in the morning!"

We both laugh, but the mirth is stilted.

Tonight is the first night we're going out together, yet apart.

See, Violet has been there for me for the past several months, supportive, loving, hiding well the pain and heartache I'm sure she feels.

A couple of weeks ago, though, she came to me and announced (not asked, not suggested) that she was going to go out herself. "After all," she joked, "it's not fair that you're the only one who gets to meet cute guys."

I laughed at that and tried to push back down in some subconscious muck the jealousy that rose up. It wasn't easy. Jealousy is not a rational emotion.

"And what would that look like?" I wondered, trying to keep my "supportive" mask firmly in place. "Singles bar?"

She cocked her head. "You do realize I've never even been in one of those places? I can't imagine!"

Violet and I had gotten engaged when we were juniors in college. I'd asked her to marry me under a famous arch on campus, notorious for its number of wedding proposals, and she'd said yes. Her dating experience, before me, was all high school stuff, pretty much, which was also my story. We were both virgins and experienced our first times together in her narrow dorm-room bed. I came too soon and thought I must be heterosexual.

"So what's your plan?"

Violet's smile is all hope and optimism—yet forced. "St. Theresa's has a singles group that meets for a potluck in the church rectory on Saturdays once a month. I'm going to go check it out." Her voice quavered a little as she told me. "I made my seven-layer salad."

"You have someone to go with?"

She looks down at the concrete floor of the patio. "No. Not really." She lifts her gaze to me, craving something—encouragement?—in return. "The point is to meet people, right?"

I nodded. Part of me wanted to say I'd go with her, but that would defeat the goal of the eventual loving uncoupling we'd been hoping for.

And now here we are, Saturday night in Chicago. Along with a bit of heat lightning and a distant rumble of thunder, there's a sense of anticipation in the air.

And fear. Not a little fear.

This is the first time both of us have gone out on our own without the other to meet other eligible people. It's weird and feels like we are lifting our feet at the same time and stepping over a giant line in the sand.

I say nothing for a while and stare out into the night. A few fireflies dance lazily at eye level. At last, I turn back to Violet and say, "You look nice."

"Thanks. You don't look so bad yourself. The running is paying off."

For some reason, I feel embarrassed at her complimenting my body since it's no longer in her purview. "I need to get dressed."

"Oh? You're not going like that? I think the boys would love it."

I smile. A few months ago, Violet could have never made such a joke. "Thanks, honey. But I think I'll be old Mr. Conservative and cover up a bit."

"Spoilsport! What time are you due there?"

"They said anytime after eight." I smile. "I know. I get too hungry for dinner at eight. I just have to live with it this time."

Violet's smile slips away and she doesn't look back. Instead, she moves to the edge of the balcony and peers to the east. "I believe my chariot is in the next block. I should go."

She turns to head for the door. At the last minute, she rushes back to give me a hug and a peck on the cheek. She feels small in my arms, like a bird, and I wonder what's in store for both of us tonight.

I PACE OUTSIDE Stephen and Rory's condo on Marine Drive, craning my neck to look up at their glittering tower. The chrome and glass high-rise faces a wide expanse of green park and then the broader, wilder expanse of Lake Michigan. Their forty-second floor view captures not only the shimmering, ever-changing waters of the lake, but also a bit of the city to the north, continuing all the way up to the campus of Northwestern University on clear days.

Since we met last spring at North End, Stephen and Rory have become my first, my best, and—as far as I know—my only gay friends. Although they'd never admit it, they've sort of taken me under their wing. I've been seeing them two or three times a month, and despite having met in a bar, we've yet to return to one. Usually, they have me over for dinner. Rory is always the cook, and he's pretty terrible, making lots of slow-cooker meals with condensed cream of mushroom soup or casseroles that involve Tater Tots, which he calls hot dish. He lived in St. Paul, Minnesota until he was fifteen and tells me hot dish is the state cuisine. I don't know if that's true, but his food, in spite of being high in sodium, fat, and calories, does have a certain homey aspect to it that I enjoy.

I like how we sit around the table for hours after a meal, drinking wine, and just talking. It reminds me of when I was a little boy and the whole family would come over for holidays. We'd all gather around our big dining room table, and my sweating mother would hover over everyone, while serving up her Sicilian specialties—things like Romano and bread-crumbed stuffed artichokes and wedding soup made with escarole, tiny meatballs, beaten egg, and pastina. My father forever beseeched her to sit down and eat, but there was always something else to attend to in the kitchen.

Like those family meals, much of the talk at Stephen and Rory's table revolves around memories. They tell me of their travels. Stephen's confinement to a wheelchair doesn't slow him down. They've been just about everywhere. New York City, Boston, LA, Santa Fe, San Francisco, Seattle...all the major cities. They've been to London, Rome, Paris, and Amsterdam. Kauai. Belize. Iceland.

Pictures and artifacts from their travels decorate their little one-bedroom aerie, competing at times with the natural and architectural splendor on display outside their floor-to-ceiling windows. What I like about their place, other than the stunning views, is that it feels so homey and lived in. For the first time, I understand how two gay men who love each other can and do constitute a family.

They've told me the story of how they met—as boys in high school. They both went to Roycemore, a Richie Rich private school in Evanston. "We were both nerds, believe it or not. I mean look at us now!" Stephen laughed. "Being different, and me a little bit of an outcast, brought us together. We bonded over books, mainly. *A Separate Peace. My Darling, My Hamburger*. Of course, *The Catcher in the Rye*."

"Don't forget the dirty parts in *The Godfather*," Rory added, laughing.

"Page twenty-eight." Stephen nodded. When I looked at him, head cocked, he explained, "That's the part where the bridesmaid takes Sonny's big salami at the wedding reception up against the bathroom door."

"We recreated that one."

They both laughed, and at the time, I didn't know if they meant it or not.

Stephen wasn't in a wheelchair back then. That didn't happen until he was in his early twenties, maybe ten years ago, as a result of a head-on collision on Sheridan Road one late weekend night. "Drunk driver," Stephen always says, as if the tragic set of circumstances no longer bothers him. "I'd bitch about it, but *I* was the drunk driver." He shakes his head. "At least the driver of the other car, a gal from Winnetka, only got some minor cuts and bruises."

Surprisingly (or not), we don't dwell on Stephen's disability. After a while with them, I barely even notice the difference, especially when we're gathered around their big dining table.

When we don't do dinners, we check out movies at the Century mall a little south of them, or go see some local theater—sometimes bigger productions at the Goodman, but we all like the smaller stuff by up-and-comers like Steppenwolf and the other little storefront theaters all over the city.

And, surprisingly, our conversation doesn't dwell on being gay—much. That's what I really like, and it's not because we *avoid* such conversation.

When I go over there, being gay simply isn't a big deal. It's just another fact, among many, that we have in common. Eye color, hair color, weight, height—all those things enter into who we are. All of those and more, things like what kind of movies we like, the types of books we read, our political beliefs, our spiritual leanings, figure into our conversations and how we relate to one another.

It's a relief to be there with them in a place where I'm safe, and being gay is just another aspect, no greater or no lesser, than any other. It's just who we are.

For someone who's hidden in the shadows almost his whole life, this indifference toward my sexual orientation is a revelation. I never dreamed my homosexuality could simply be no big deal.

Stephen and Rory, in their own quiet way, have demonstrated that there's no shame in being who you are. Crusty Stephen would say there's no honor in it, either, and he's right.

I just am. Just like everyone else. My actions and how I treat myself and others determine my worth, not the fact that I prefer sausage over pie.

TONIGHT, THOUGH, I'M skittish, part of me believing my evening would be better spent at a Denny's counter, having a piece of banana cream pie and a coffee.

Before going in through the revolving doors and smiling at the doorman who looks like Ken Olin, I need to compose myself. Question myself. Is this zinfandel the right wine? Do the flowers I picked up at Dominick's look cheap? Are the cargo shorts and simple black T dressy enough?

I'm anxious because Stephen and Rory, for the first time, have invited a fourth for dinner. A young guy close to my age who they'd met during comedy night at Sidetracks the week before.

"It's not a fix up," Rory assures me.

"We'd never play matchmaker," Stephen says. "You're a big boy. You can bring down your own game."

I'm not so sure.

But I'm here now.

And the future awaits...way up high in the sky.

STEPHEN'S SEATED BY the window in the living room, his chair angled toward the North Side cityscape and its towers of lights, a boxy glass of Scotch in his hand. I'd asked him once about drinking, not long after we met. "I mean, you're in a wheelchair because of being drunk," I'd said. "I would've guessed you wouldn't want anything to do with alcohol now."

He'd nodded. "See, the thing is and was—I'm not an alcoholic. I'm not even a big drinker, in the final analysis. I was young and drunk, like a lot of us are when we're in our early twenties, rebelling, thinking we're cool. It was one sad night for me. Unfortunate. But the accident and what followed wasn't a result of a pattern even if it was a result of being drunk. You know what I mean? No, the lesson I learned was that I could drink socially and responsibly, but never a drop if I'm going to be driving."

Yes, Stephen can drive his specially-equipped car and does so quite well.

He smiles and raises his glass as I slip in through the door they've left open a crack for me. "Welcome! Did you have any sixty-second romances on the way over?"

Sixty-second romances are what I call those moments on the L train when you meet the gaze of another man and hold it for just a little longer than a casual glance. Both of you understand, in those few seconds, that something electric is passing between you. And then you move on, thus the sixty-second romance. Now that I'm aware of them, I have them all the time, at all hours of the day and night. But I've never been bold enough to do anything more than look. And even when that gets too intense, I find myself staring down at the floor, heat rising to my cheeks.

"Unfortunately, no. All I saw was a crazy lady with what looked like all her belongings stuffed into a couple of Aldi bags. She was rambling on and on about 'you and your damn Swedish Bakery cookies.'"

"Funny?"

"Not at all," I tell Stephen, moving across the living room to sit down beside him. "She was sad. I think she saw so many people in that car that I couldn't. Riding the L is always entertaining, I have to say."

"And scary." He downs his scotch and asks me if I'll have the usual. "Hon!" he calls, "Would you mind fixing me one more and whipping up a G & T for Randy here?"

I'd heard the soft murmur of voices coming from the kitchen when I entered, and they abruptly stopped when Stephen called out. I could also smell something burning, but I've let go any hopes of having decent food when I come over here.

It's all about the atmosphere.

Rory pokes his head out from the kitchen. "Hey Randy! Come on out here and make them yourself, okay? I can't leave the stove."

I smile, glad to be included in things—it's so much easier than sitting around and making small talk.

In their little, white galley kitchen, Rory is pulling down a clean glass for me from the cupboard. There's already a bottle of Tanqueray and one of Glenfiddich on the counter.

And there's a man standing at the stove, back to me, his arm motions indicating he's stirring something. His shoulders are broad, testing the seams of his red T-shirt. His biceps look like hams. Thick black curls crown a solid head, bent over a steaming pan. I'd be lying if I said I didn't notice his taut ass and broad thighs, both shown off nicely in worn, faded denim. He's barefoot and this simple exposure of skin tantalizes me more than I think it should. I have to tear my eyes away from his feet on the pale hardwood.

Rory taps him on the shoulder. "Turn around and meet our other guest."

Rory takes his place at the stove, while the guy dries off his hands on a dishtowel hanging from the refrigerator handle.

He turns and smiles. I know him from somewhere, but no bells have sounded just yet.

Yet he recognizes me, judging from the way his dark-brown eyes light up when he sees me, from the broadness of his grin. "Hey!" he says, beaming. He comes toward me, hand extended. "It's you again."

His hand is big, raw, calloused, and his grip so hard it almost makes me go weak in the knees. Our eyes lock as we shake hands, and I wonder if he's thinking the same thing as I am— *Why are we shaking hands when a kiss would be so much better?* Surely, he's *not* thinking that, right? But I'm a half-full kind of guy.

"I keep running into you," he says. "First at Sidetrack last winter, and then you had the bad luck to come across me a couple months ago, fighting with one of my beaus. Lord! But it's good to see you." His voice and the unbridled joy in his face bring out a smile in me too.

And, without effort, everything clicks into place. I remember. Even that very terrified night at Sidetrack when I stepped into my first gay bar.

It's flattering and kind of mind-boggling that he remembers seeing me so well.

Yet for the life of me, I can't say what his name is. I hope if I remind him of mine, he'll tell me his. "I'm Randy. Randy Kay."

"Like Special K?"

"Very." I wait for him to supply his name. I stop holding my breath. I pour drinks, making myself a gin and tonic, a scotch, neat, for Stephen, and beers (Rolling Rock) for the two men in the kitchen with me.

As I hand him his beer, he finally ends the suspense. "I'm John Walsh." Our fingers meet over the sweating green glass of the beer bottle, which causes our eyes to lock again. The gaze is more, I swear, intimate than a kiss.

Rory is watching. "Looks like you boys will get along. And you have a history too. How nice!" He takes Stephen's scotch from the counter and grabs his own beer. In the doorway from the kitchen, he pauses. "Would it be terribly rude of me to ask you two to finish up the dinner prep?" He puts a hand to his forehead. "I'm tired."

I laugh. "Sure, Rory. We'll see how we can improve on it."

"Hey!"

"Go on. Get out of here." I want to add, but I'm not so presumptuous that I know he's pushing John and I together, protests that this is not a fix up aside.

John returns to the pan on the stove, moving dark and darker bits of meat and vegetable around with a spatula.

I move close to peer over his shoulder. "What is that?"

John turns to me, his face close, and grimaces. "Rory said hash. Some kind of hash. Roast beast?" He sets down the spatula to point to a couple of blackened cubes. "That's supposed to be some of the beef, left over from Sunday's dinner."

"And those? Potatoes? Onions? Carrots?"

"You'd think. But it's hard to say for sure." He turns off the gas. "More heat is not going to improve this." He sets down his spatula and leans against the sink, taking a swig of his beer. "How do you know the guys?"

I tell him about our encounter at North End a while back and explain how they've sort of taken me under their wing.

"Sort of like gay godfathers?"

I laugh. "You could say that." Suddenly, there's a rushing in my head. My heart feels as if it's fluttering like a hummingbird's wings. There's something about the way John stands, casually holding his beer, that looks, well, beautiful to me. I don't know how he'd like having the word "beauty" ascribed to him, but it fits better than the more manly compliments like handsome or hunky. John has his legs crossed and it forces up and out that faded denim bulge very, um, fetchingly. He catches me looking once and grins.

Of course, my face feels like it's on fire.

"How did you meet Stephen and Rory?"

"Ah, they were a little friendlier than you were at Sidetrack." He laughs. "I'm just giving you shit. You probably don't even remember, but I tried to buy you a beer. You rushed out of the bar like I offered you a turd."

If any more heat rises to my cheeks, I'm afraid my face will explode. "Gee, I'm sorry."

John laughs and claps a hand on my shoulder and gives it a squeeze. The touch is electric, stirring me in ways I would have before thought impossible from such a simple gesture. I find myself a little breathless and at a loss for words.

"You don't have to apologize. You looked scared. And that made me feel sorry for you. I just wanted to be a friend because it looked like you needed one."

"That's so kind of you." The lust I felt a moment ago switches to gratitude and a different kind of appreciation for this guy.

He waves my comment away. "It was nothing. I'm not Mother Teresa either. I'd be lying if I didn't admit to ulterior motives." He grins and gives me a little wink, which sends a shiver down my spine.

"I wish I would have taken that drink. I wish we would have talked." And I do. But I wasn't ready. Not that night. Not even close.

Tonight, maybe I'm ready. I regard John's dark chocolate eyes and think I see in them a depth that goes beyond mere lust—either within me or within him.

"Well, why didn't you?"

I realize John knows nothing about me or my history. I'm about to launch into the whole long story of my upbringing, Catholicism, small-town values, early marriage, early fatherhood, and more, when Stephen saves me from embarrassment by rolling into the kitchen.

Nearly smashing my toes in the process, he crosses the small space to peer into the nonstick skillet on the stove. "Jesus Christ," he whispers. "Hey Rory! Honey?"

Rory pokes his head in the kitchen. "Yes, dear?"

Stephen smiles and points to the hash. "You know what? This looks great, but I'm really having a taste for pizza tonight. Would you mind if we ordered in from Giordano's?" He makes a good effort at looking somewhat helpless and wanting to please. He eyes us. "You guys wouldn't mind pizza, would you?"

John speaks up. "I don't know. That hash is making my mouth water."

And I'm recalling how my mouth often waters just before I throw up. I stay quiet.

"Well, if you really want pizza, Stephen, we can have pizza. I'll go call in the order. In the meantime, why don't you refresh these boys' drinks? They look like they could use some cooling down."

It's only after Rory leaves the kitchen I notice how close John and I are standing.

Stephen eyes us as he gets more alcohol. "Really guys. We seldom meet anyone out at the bars that we want to invite over for dinner, but you two charmed us both. The fact that we've invited you on the same night doesn't mean anything. No pressure." Stephen looks at me, then at John. "I know you both have your issues."

John shrugs. "Who, me? I got no issues. I got no baggage."

"That's good to hear," I tell him. Already, I wonder if my having a wife and kid at home will send him screaming off into the night. I wouldn't blame him if it did.

"I call bullshit." Stephen hands a fresh bottle of Rolling Rock to John. "You have issues just like this one over here." And he turns to hand me a fresh gin and tonic.

I exchange a questioning glance with John that Stephen notices. "But I will leave you two to your own devices to discover what issues you have. Also what benefits you bring to the table." He grins and exits the kitchen.

We bump glass and bottle. "Is this our first date?" I ask and immediately feel like a dork. I have a lot to learn. Being new to being gay is enough, but I also haven't dated *anyone* in years.

John cocks his head. "No. This is dinner with mutual friends." He leans close. "And thank God, we don't have to eat roast beast hash."

We both chuckle, but I can't help feeling disappointed, which surprises me.

"But we can have a date tomorrow night, if you're up for it. And available."

Immediately, Violet's face appears in my mind's eye. *Two night's in a row? I can hear her asking. So this is how it's starting to go?* She's hurt, maybe a little surprised. Should I tell John I have to check with the wife first? At that thought, I burst into a very unflattering giggle.

"Hey!" John throws up defensive hands. "Just never mind. Usually, they don't laugh at me until we get in the bedroom." He moves close. "Thanks for saving me the time."

I have to rein in my laughter. "No, no. I'm not laughing at you." I try to regulate my breathing back to normal, to wipe that grin off my face. Poor guy. "I was just laughing because I've never—" I don't know how to put it. I'm in my early thirties, young and healthy. People say I'm cute. "I've never—" I swallow.

"Never what? I'm pretty vanilla, so don't worry that I'm too jaded for you or anything."

"I've just never been on a date with a man." I say the words in a rush, knowing what they will imply to him— that I'm married or at least buried at the back of the closet. I look down suddenly, and yes, of course I'm wearing it. The gold band on my left hand glints in the illumination from the track lighting.

"A looker like you?" John asks, surprised. He then, as though my mind directed him to it, glances down at the ring on my finger. It comes together for him; I can see it as the puzzle pieces fall into place. "Ah...you're married."

I nod. "Got a kid too. A little boy, Henry. He's gonna be six."

John smiles but there's a yearning ache in it; in his eyes too. "It all makes sense now."

"That night at Sidetrack?"

He nods.

"First time out for me."

"No wonder you were scared."

"I was petrified."

"No, first you were afraid, *then* you were petrified."

My eyebrows come together in confusion. "What?"

"Nothin'. Pop culture reference. You'll get it once you're out longer."

I stand with him in silence, nervously sipping. I wonder if the magic spell has broken, if this changes everything. We hear the sound of the phone ringing and Rory answering, telling the doorman-who-looks-like-Ken-Olin to "send him right on up."

"Pizza's here," John tells me and then leaves the room.

My heart sinks. I don't have the nerve to call out to him, "So is the offer of that date still on the table?"

I follow, very much doubting his invitation will stand. Why should it? I've been out enough (even in my own shy, limited capacity) to know that he's got scores of hot, young, *unmarried* men to choose from. Why saddle himself with me and my problems?

I wish he would.

As I follow him, I tell myself I need to be ready for things not working out the way I want them to. I may need to explore that group I noticed in the *Reader* classifieds last week—the one that was looking for gay married men to meet up for coffee and "fellowship" at a straight café in Wrigleyville. The prospect seemed kind of depressing and off-putting to me—a bunch of guys with wives. Would I never move beyond being gay and married?

"Pizza! Pizza!" Rory cries as he throws open the door.

I plant a smile on my face and join everybody at the dining room table where Stephen's already laid out paper napkins, Chinet, and glasses of Chianti.

THE EVENING DIDN'T go as awkwardly as I thought. In fact, after a few glasses of wine and a couple slices, I found myself laughing, hard, at the conversation. We move into the living room and watch a videotape, *Young Frankenstein*, which allows the laughter to continue.

It also gives John the freedom to sit close, the sides of our bodies touching. My hard-on waxed and waned, and I couldn't believe how erotic the sides of two bodies, fully clothed, touching could be.

Toward the end of the evening, after the movie, and the cutlery and glasses are in the dishwasher, Rory and Stephen headed off to bed, telling John and me to just pull the door closed behind us when we leave. "You boys behave." Stephen shakes a finger at us. "I don't want to have poor Rory cleaning come stains off the couch in the morning."

Rory just shakes his head. "Jesus, honey."

Before heading off, they'd turned off most of the lights in the condo. Mood setting? Energy conservation? I don't know and I don't care. Suddenly, I'm alone in a cocoon of dim and quiet with John Walsh.

And I can't think of a single thing to say.

After a time, John turns to me. "So, a married guy?"

I nod. There's that feeling again of being caught between two worlds and belonging in neither. It makes me sad because I'm growing to like this guy a lot—*Is this what a gay crush feels like?*—and I suppose my marital status will eventually interfere with the two of us forming any kind of significant bond.

We're still on the couch. I nudge his shoulder with mine. "Is that a problem? Really?" I want to circle back to him asking me out. It's been on my mind the whole night.

He locks his gaze with my own. "Not unless it's a problem for you. Let me ask you this—where do things stand with you and, uh, the wife?"

I blow out a sigh. What do I say here? Do I tell him it's complicated? What can I say that won't send him scurrying away? There's no right answer, so I eventually decide on the truth. "We're working on things. She's a great woman—probably far too understanding than I have a right to expect." I pause to gnaw my lower lip for just a moment. I think of Violet out at the church social and wonder if she's met any men. She's good-looking—blond, beautiful figure—I know she'll stand out. Will someone approach her? Has someone approached her already? The questions cause a wave of queasiness to rise up in my gut. Completely illogical and certainly not justifiable, but it's my heart that's sending an ache to my gut, not my head.

And yet...I still want to grasp at a chance with this guy sitting next to me.

I look down and then back up at him. "Look. The truth is we love each other. We always have. And we still do. We made a sweet boy together, and for better or worse, that little life will always keep us connected, no matter what. Violet knows I need to be true to who I am." I stop, thinking of how close I came to suicide last winter, and the memory makes me shudder.

"But I'm ready to explore. To see what this world has to offer me."

"The gay world?" John snorts and rolls his eyes. "Hate to tell you this, bud. But the prospects on Planet Queer are pretty grim." His face kind of collapses into despair, and I can't hold back. I touch his cheek for the briefest of moments, and he grabs my hand and squeezes it before letting go. I sit back, my hands in my lap.

John goes on. "I'm sorry. I shouldn't say things like that to a newbie." He shrugs. "I've just been very unlucky in love."

"You?" I ask in surprise.

"Yes. You flatter me. Thanks. But it's true. Sex is easy. Love is a whole 'nother story."

We sit for a while in the quiet and the dim. I feel him close to me, and it sends a surge to both my heart and my groin. I want to do more—to reach out, to hold him, to kiss him, to drop to my knees between those denim-clad thighs, tug at his zipper and—" *Whoa! Where's that shit coming from?*

In the end, I say simply, "The wife wants me to meet a nice man. Someone she knows won't hurt me. Someone she can feel safe knowing that when he meets our Henry, it will be okay."

John nods. I can't tell what he's thinking. "I don't know if I can make promises."

I nod.

And we go quiet once again. I make a move to stand. I want to go look out the window at the city lights, distract myself from a conversation that's grown too serious for a casual dinner with friends.

John lightly grabs hold of my wrist. "You're not getting ready to go, are you?"

"No. I just wanted to partake of the incredible view just over there."

I move toward the wall of glass. Outside, city lights shimmer like gilded towers, and I think how much I love this city perched at the edge of a vast lake. I press my forehead to the cool glass and close my eyes.

As I stand there, I feel John come up behind me. The feel of his hands on my shoulders awaken something within me—a kind of pulse that synchronizes with the beat of my heart.

He nears and whispers. "I didn't want you to leave yet because I haven't had a chance to kiss you."

A chill runs down my spine. I turn to him.

We're in each other's arms, bodies pressed close. I think, for only a moment, how different a man feels in my arms than a woman—bigger, more solid, almost oppressive, and yet protective and warm.

The best word, though?

Right. This feels *right*.

Gently, he takes my chin in his hand, positioning my face toward his, and he leans in to kiss me. I lose myself in the warmth of him, the taste of his lips, of his tongue. The sweetness of him married to the pizza and wine we had earlier. I begin to shake and hate myself for it. My knees go weak, and I feel like I could pass out.

He must notice because he pulls me tighter to him. We don't stop kissing. Our passion rises, and I can feel his excitement next to my own as our hips grind together. This is dirty, sweet, and sublime all at once.

Finally, he pulls away to look me in the eye. I let out a quivering breath, grateful that I didn't come in my pants. I was almost there.

And he says the words I've been longing to hear, "Tomorrow night, then? Dinner?"

I can only nod. I feel emptied out and filled up. I feel like jumping for joy and leaping from a ledge. I feel as though I've never been this alive before.

"Yes," I say. "Yes."

And I lean in to kiss *him*.

Chapter Eleven

RANDY

The warmth of John's lips still clings to my own as I step off the L train at the Jarvis stop. I hurry down the steps, trying not to note how the concrete stairway smells of pee, and hurry outside.

A light rain has begun to fall and the mist reminds me of a poem where the poet compares the lightness of the precipitation to a kiss. In my mood, it seems fitting. The streetlamps wear a caul of gray. I can hear, even from here, the hiss of car tires east of me on busy Sheridan Road.

Jarvis is quiet at just before eleven o'clock. There's a gay bar on the corner, Charmers, and I can tell it's doing a lively business at this hour. A couple guys, older men, both wearing baseball caps, T-shirts, and jeans, exit the bar on a wave of disco music courtesy of Donna Summer, laughter, chatter, and a bright flash of light. They don't notice me under the L tracks, but hurry north on Greenview Avenue.

I wonder if the couple has been together for a long time or if they just met tonight and are hurrying to one of their apartments for an encounter.

John and I had talked, before we parted, of my coming to his place to spend the night. And I was ready, honestly. But he said something that still makes me catch my breath. "I don't want a one-nighter with you. You're special. I want our first time to be out of the ordinary, memorable. You know?"

I did know, in spite of the half of a hard-on that stubbornly refused to go away even though we'd stopped kissing. And I was flattered that he wanted to wait. I didn't think this was the typical modus operandi for gay men.

I walk slowly through the chilling mist, wondering how I'll tell Violet that I have a date for the next night, my first ever with a man. I don't want to cause her any pain, and my excitement and anticipation are tempered by how she might react.

But when I open the door to our little apartment, I find that I'll have to wait to tell Violet my news.

The apartment is dark, save for the small lamp we have on a table behind the couch. It's soft cone of light projects upward, leaving our living room a place of shadows.

The emptiness is odd, almost unsettling. In the vacuum of Henry not being there, the place is too quiet and feels like someone else's home. I will need to go downstairs in a minute to Mrs. Roberts and pick him up.

But where is Violet? I consult my watch and see that's it's now a quarter after eleven. I tell myself that a church social shouldn't go this late. Is she okay? Nausea, unwarranted and illogical, rises up to irritate me, like a buzzing gnat in my ear. Am I really worried about her welfare? Or am I more worried that she's met a man at this social and is right now with him somewhere, perhaps engaged in the same kind of kissing I just experienced.

The shock of the thought makes my mouth dry. I sit for a moment on the couch. I tell myself she's probably still at the church hall, or she met another young woman and the two went out somewhere for a nightcap and to compare stories about why they find themselves at a church singles mixer.

I get up, shaking my head, telling myself I have no right to worry that Violet has met a man. After all, so have I.

Still, I think I pushed the thought away that she might have her own needs, that she might need the comfort of a *straight* guy as balm to her wounds, wounds that I've inflicted.

As I turn on a few more lights in the apartment, I try to stem the tide of guilt I feel rising up within me. This guilt is something I've worked hard to banish over the past few months, with quiet moments alone, trying to understand myself better, and with my therapist, who leads me to the indisputable truth that guilt is a worthless emotion, one that can only retard my growth.

I go in Henry's room and turn down the quilt his grandmother back in Ohio made for him when he was born—all stars and planets on a navy blue field—to reveal his beloved pale blue flannel sheets that he can't bear to part with even though it's getting warmer.

I put on the little lamp on his nightstand with its multicolored, translucent shade.

The L rumbles by outside.

Mrs. Roberts answers the door even before I knock. She must have heard my footfall on the stairs.

Her smile warms me. "He's out like a light," she says.

In direct contradiction, Henry sits up on the couch and rubs his eyes. "No, I ain't!" he says cheerfully.

Mrs. Roberts turns to him, "No, I'm *not*," she corrects.

Henry swings his legs off the couch, looking abashed. "Sorry, Ms. Roberts."

She goes over to him and pulls the throw that was covering him off.

My little boy is revealed. Striped T-shirt, jeans with the cuffs rolled, bare feet. If he isn't the cutest little boy in the world, I don't know who is.

Henry hops down from the couch. Mrs. Roberts brings him his red Chuck Taylors and squats to put them on.

He shoos her away. "I can do it," he says with my lack of patience.

"Of course you can, little guy." She stands again and looks over her shoulder to grin at me.

"Where's Mama?" Henry stands once he has his shoes on and tied (a new skill for him and one he's proud of).

Mrs. Roberts eyes me, too, waiting for an answer. I often come down alone to pick up Henry when she babysits, but I think she, at least, can discern that something's a little off tonight.

I'm not sure what to tell him, so I just say, "She'll be home soon." I pull out my wallet and take out a couple of bills to pay Mrs. Roberts. Her menagerie of dogs and cats have now come fully awake. A cat makes a figure eight against my calves, purring. One of the dogs rushes to the door.

I tug on Henry's hand. "Come on, we need you to get back to slumberland. They'll wonder where you've gotten to."

We've always referred to Henry's sleep as a special place, populated by all different sorts of people and creatures. He believes, and maybe he's right, that there's little difference between the real world and what we call the dream one. Wise kid, right?

We march up the stairs, quiet.

Inside the apartment, Henry dashes through the living room and dining room to the kitchen. He checks the bathroom and the room his mother now sleeps in, as though he didn't believe me downstairs when I told him she'd be home soon.

"She's not here, buddy. But I expect she'll walk through that door just about any minute."

I lead him to the bathroom and supervise the brushing of teeth and the drinking of water. In his room, I undress Henry and put on his blue pj's with their penguin design. Finally, I tuck him into bed and lean down to kiss his forehead.

"No story?" he asks, a hopeful glint in his eye. He rolls on his side to stare pointedly at *Where the Wild Things Are*, which is on his nightstand. Violet or I have read him the book, gosh, at least a million times.

I shake my head and attempt a stern, fatherly look. I'm sure I fail. But I back it up with the simple pronouncement, "It's late. Get to sleep."

"Can I keep my night-light on?"

"Sure."

I head out from his room, closing the door behind me. I expect Henry to call out to leave the door open, but he doesn't.

I plop down on the couch, think about getting out the sheets, pillow, and blanket I keep in the hallway linen closet. When Henry asked why I'd been sleeping on the couch, we told him Daddy snores too much, and it keeps Mama awake and he buys it.

When will we need to tell him something more truthful? When I finally get up the courage and resources to leave? Or when Violet gives up and throws me out...as she has every right to.

I stay on the couch for a while, remembering my evening with the boys...and John. It should make me happy, but I can't help wondering where Violet is.

It's now after midnight.

I know I won't sleep until she comes home. It's irrational, yes, but I can't help it. I also can't quell the nausea in my gut, which is putting a damper on the thrill and optimism I ended the evening with earlier.

At last, I get up and walk to Henry's door. I crack it open. He's asleep, burrowed under the covers so that only his forehead and his mop of dark curls show. He's snoring lightly. The colors in the room shift from blue to red to yellow. I envy him the innocence of his world and wonder what harm I'll do to him eventually.

I shake my head, telling myself not to think like that. I close the door to his room, holding the knob so there's no telltale click to wake him. The doorway to our balcony is only a few steps, and I quickly head outside, leaving the balcony door open in case Henry should wake and call out for me.

Outside, the air has gotten even cooler, and the mist I walked home in has turned to rain. I sit on the ledge and overlook our street. The leaves rustle in the breeze. The rain makes a soft hissing noise. It should be pleasant, soothing, but I'm worried.

Where is she? Is she okay? What's she doing right now?

I vacillate between worrying that she's hurt, in a car accident or something, and fearing that she's just the opposite and her absence and the late hour indicate not that's she's in trouble, but that she's having a very good time.

Even though I know it shouldn't, the latter notion wounds me. And the later the hour goes, the sicker I feel.

You have no right!

Every car that approaches makes my hope rise, especially if the car is a taxi. But the hope slumps back down as the cars pass our building, not stopping or even slowing. Once one does, a beat-up pickup with a noisy muffler. I watch silently as our neighbor from upstairs, a young man just out of Northwestern, gets out, stumbling. I watch him trip and fall on the verge of grass in front of our apartment building, thinking I should do something, call down a helpful word, but then think better of it as he laughs at himself and gets up to come inside.

I get cold. I notice my chill only because I'm shivering. I shouldn't be shivering—it's summer for crying out loud! Welcome to Chicago.

I go back in, put the TV on, and turn the volume to low. I just happen to land on a movie halfway through, *Mildred Pierce*, with Joan Crawford. I try to interest myself in the story, but my mind keeps wandering back outdoors, thinking I've heard a car stopping out front. Every passage of an L train makes me think I should get up and return to the balcony, where I will see my wayward wife in the orangish glow of a street light, coming up Ashland Avenue.

But at last, all I do is fall asleep, just as things are getting really melodramatic in the movie.

I AWAKE SUDDENLY as images from my dream disperse—something about walking down a long tunnel, with hooded figures either waiting for me or chasing me; I can't recall which. I look around the living room, feeling disoriented and groggy, as though I just spent the previous night heavily drinking. The TV is still on, but now it's some infomercial and they're roasting a chicken in half the time it would take in the oven. I snag the remote off the coffee table and turn the TV off.

Silence rushes in. The clock on our cable box tells me it's just after four a.m. Switching the television off not only took away any noise, but also the light. The room is blanketed in a kind of murky darkness, augmented by the streetlight outside. The furniture morphs into menacing shadows, beasts that could come alive.

I force myself to sit up, the throw I'd pulled over myself at some unremembered point slithering off me to puddle on the hardwood floor. There's a crick in my neck, and at this weird hour when the world seems to have gone silent, the atmosphere in our apartment just seems off somehow, impossible to describe.

I feel alone.

I get to my feet as the hope rises that Violet has come home while I was sleeping. *Sure, she has. She just didn't want to wake you and went into bed as quietly as possible.*

I head toward what used to be our bedroom at the rear of the apartment. I pause at the closed door and whisper a little prayer to myself that she's in there, tangled up in the bed clothes, sleeping.

I turn the doorknob and open the door very slowly, so it doesn't creak.

The room doesn't face the street and the blinds are shut, so the room is filled with a darkness so thick it feels palpable.

I don't hear movement. I don't hear her breathing. Holding my hands out in front of me, I move into the room until my knees bump our bed. Um, *her* bed. I feel around on the smooth surface of the comforter, and even in the dark, I can tell the bed is made.

Sighing, I switch on the small lamp on the nightstand. No surprises here. The bed is pristine, the room mockingly empty.

I take in all the familiar stuff—her makeup and jewelry scattered haphazardly across the dresser, the tubes, bottles, and pots that are a mystery to me as a man. One drawer hangs open and in it, I can see a pile of panties, in all different colors, some lacy and sexy, others more utilitarian.

I wonder what she chose to wear tonight.

I rifle through the drawer, wondering if something's hidden there, but I find nothing. I know I shouldn't do it, but I open the other drawers in the dresser. Half of these drawers, before my revelation last winter, used to be mine. Violet's filled them with her own things—bras, shorts for summer, T-shirts and tank tops, scarves, gloves, and mittens. One drawer is what my mom used to call a "junk drawer." In it, there's a tangled mess of CDs, a small spiral-bound notebook, receipts from grocery stores and restaurants. Old keys. Matchbooks. Photographs in a little pile in one corner.

I pull these out and move to the bed to sit down with them. I smile as I look through the bittersweet memories these represent—there's Henry, age two, and me at Lincoln Park Zoo. He's on my shoulders so he can get a better view of the giraffes. Here's Violet and me one New Year's Eve two or three years ago, having dinner at a French restaurant downtown, Le Perroquet, that we both thought was overpriced and pretentious. A family shot at Six Flags Great America in front of a carousel. Henry's three in this one, and he holds aloft a cloud of pink cotton candy. More snapshots, more memories, bringing both smiles and tears.

And then I come across one I don't recognize. It sends a jolt through me.

For one, it's black and white, but not old, just more artsy than anything we would have taken. A man stands on the trail heading into downtown, near Fullerton Avenue, where it really opens up to display Chicago's incredible skyline. I can see a bit of the lake, throwing spray up as it crashes against the shoreline.

The man is handsome. Salt-and-pepper hair and a big mustache. He reminds me of the actor Sam Elliot. I pause as another thought occurs to me, and it makes me gasp— he also reminds me of an older version of myself. I stare at him, the grin on his face, the pale gray of his eyes. He's dressed in a black sweater and black jeans, combat boots. His thick hair is messed up—fetchingly—by the wind off the lake. He's looking right into the lens of the camera, and it makes it hard to look away, his gaze is so intense.

Who the hell is he?

Again, that totally irrational swell of jealousy flares. I tell myself this could be someone from Violet's past before she even knew me. It could even be a relative, someone I never met at the family reunions in the summertime up at Lake Geneva in Wisconsin. Hell, she might not even know this guy, but might have found the photograph lost or discarded somewhere, topping the trash in a public can or on the floor of a L train car. He could be a coworker.

All of these rational answers don't convince me. What my heart tells me is that this is someone Violet has met, probably recently, and is involved with.

Something tells me this is who she's with tonight.

I put the pictures back where I found them and slam the drawer they were in too hard.

I switch off the light and leave the room. I head back through the living room and outside once more, to stand and overlook the street from our balcony.

Violet, oh Violet, where are you?

The sky is at last beginning to lighten, almost imperceptibly. It's just slightly less dark and grayer than it was, signaling that dawn is on its way, not far behind. The air is warmer now that the rain has stopped. There's a damp smell—earth and vegetation.

I close my eyes and sit on the balcony's concrete edge. I sniffle a little and allow a couple of tears to fall. They feel crawly, ticklish on my face. I tell myself I'm being stupid and unreasonable.

Isn't this what you wanted?

I open my eyes to find the sky has grown an even paler shade of gray. A fishy-smelling breeze blows up, off the lake, and makes the leaves rustle.

I sense it before it happens: a cab rolls up in front of our building, slows, and then stops.

I wait breathlessly, knowing, knowing.

After a couple of suspense-filled minutes, the back door opens, the interior light comes on and there's Violet. She opens the door and steps out, clutching the raincoat she wore around her front.

She looks up, and even in this wan light, even from this distance, our gazes lock.

I will remember this moment forever. There's a sadness to it, the sense of things that were hurtling toward an ending at last arriving there.

My heart swells with a bittersweet kind of love, and I stand, continuing to look down at her. She makes no attempt to move, simply standing there near a parked Nissan Sentra, staring upward.

What do I see in her gaze? Is it defiance? Sadness? Guilt?

Am I projecting?

I turn at last and head into the house. I move quickly to the bathroom and close and lock the door behind me. I run the bathtub water so it will cover the sound of my tears.

I wait.

When I come out at last, the light is brighter, and Violet has gone into her room. The door is closed. When I gently try the handle, I discover it's locked.

Chapter Twelve

JOHN

Randy waits for me at Ann Sather's, a Swedish restaurant down the street from the Belmont L stop. He's slouched inside the entrance, wearing black jeans, a black T-shirt, and a black baseball cap. The black makes a sharp contrast with his olive complexion.

Rain pours down in sheets. Belmont Avenue is a parking lot of cars with their headlights turned on prematurely against the dark gray skies. Exhaust fumes, damp, and garbage rise up. Ah, summer in Chicago.

I hurry along, getting drenched because I left my umbrella at home. The damn weatherman said cloudy, not rainy.

Randy doesn't see me, and once again, he looks scared. I sigh a bit inwardly. *I thought we'd gotten past that.* There's a crowd clustered around him, waiting to be seated, yet Randy stands out, partly because of all the black he's wearing and partly because he seems so ill at ease.

I hurry inside, resisting the impulse to shake myself off like a dog. I sidle up to Randy, who seems startled by my appearance beside him.

"Didn't you get the memo?" I joke with him. "This is a Swedish restaurant now, not a funeral home." Ann Sather is perhaps the only restaurant in Chicago housed in what used to be the final stop before the grave. The idea sometimes gives me the willies, especially about eating here, but the food's too good to let it bother me *that* much.

He smiles, but the smile doesn't quite reach his dark eyes, which seem as clouded and troubled as the skies outside. "Hmm? Oh, all the black? Yeah, I put these on without thinking. Black makes that possible. The not thinking. I wasn't in the mood for thought."

I nod, unsure what to say. I hope our first date will go better than this awkward start. If he wasn't in the mood for *thought*, what else will he not be in the mood for? I had planned on hugging him, maybe even planting a kiss on those cute Cupid's bow lips, but I am picking up on a signal that tells me to keep back.

"I already put our name in for a table. We shouldn't have much of a wait." He eyes me up and down. "You want me to ask the hostess for a towel?"

"That's okay." I reach out with my tongue to snag a heavy drop of rainwater heading south from my upper lip. I slip out of my denim jacket and already feel a little drier.

A young guy with black hair, dark eyes, and a bewitching smile comes to seat us. He puts us at a table in the back, against the hand-painted wall, as though he knows this is a first date. And maybe he does.

"Carly will be your server. And she'll bring you the dinner-spoiling bread basket." He winks at me.

We laugh. If you're from Chicago, you know what that basket contains—not only an assortment of homemade breads and rolls, including limpa, but also the restaurant's famous cinnamon rolls, which are as huge as they are delicious.

When the basket comes, we split a cinnamon roll and discuss what we'll have. Randy's going for the traditional

Swedish meatballs, and I order the Tom Turkey dinner. I joke that neither of us will be able to walk out of here later, let alone be up for anything more romantic. "Loosening our belts will be to relieve the pressure, not for anything else." I think my little joke, and hint, is pretty cute.

Randy doesn't, I guess. He stares down at his plate as if he hasn't heard me.

I touch the back of his hand. "Hey. Is everything okay?"

When he meets my gaze, I can tell he's waging an internal war. A good guess on my part would be that he's trying to decide how much to share with me, especially on a first date and what may be, for him, a first *gay* date.

His shoulders relax a bit. "I'm sorry, John. I wish I was, uh, more in the mood for tonight." He shoves his half-eaten plate of food away, and then, to further make his point, takes his napkin off his lap and throws it over the meatballs and noodles.

"Hey, don't cover it up. I'll eat that." I pull his plate toward me and dig in. One of the blessings of being a big, beefy guy who works with the fire department is that I have an insane daily calorie count—or so I tell myself. It's obvious that, even though the mood at the table is tense, it doesn't affect my appetite, not when there are unwanted Swedish meatballs facing me.

But my appetite doesn't mean I'm not concerned about what Randy's just said. "What's the matter? You can share anything with me, man." And I mean it.

His gaze is faraway. A less astute observer might say he's looking over the big crowd in the dining room, but I can tell he's not seeing anything other than, perhaps, what's in his mind's eye.

He gives me a wavering smile. "It's nothing. Bad day at work. And maybe I'm just a little tired."

Normally, on a first date, I'd let it go at that, figuring the guy would tell me what's going on when he's ready. And maybe the truth would be I just wouldn't care that much as long as it didn't impede my getting in the dude's pants later on. But Randy has already worked his way into my heart. I ache when he aches even if I don't know the reason.

"Really? I know we're new to each other, but you can talk to me, Randy."

I can see the question on his face, wondering if he really can. And it makes me want to reach across the table and caress his face. It makes me want to call our waitress over, pay the check, and take him out of here to my place, so I can comfort him by holding him close, by whispering that everything will be all right even though I don't have a clue at this point what's bothering him.

Everything is *always* all right again. Until it's not. It's the way of the world.

His next words make me believe he's reading my mind. "Can we get out of here?"

I smile. "Sure. You want to see my place? It ain't much, but I have a nice bottle of Jack Daniels in the cupboard and some Stella Artois in the fridge. I think we could both use a little meeting with Jack and Stella, don't you?"

He nods and the gratitude I read on his face makes me smile.

"THIS IS NICE." Randy takes in the living room of my tiny apartment.

"You're lying. But thank you."

I look around my place, trying to see it through his eyes. I've been told it's a typical bachelor pad more than once. One guy even said my sad little home was a turn-on. "You didn't get the interior decorating gene, and I'm so glad," he'd said before unloosening my belt and yanking at the buttons on my Levi 501s.

I don't know about an interior decorator gene, but my home does reflect me and I'm all about comfort. I couldn't care less about pretense, Feng Shui, or the latest trends in decor. My red-and-gray striped couch is from Goodwill, but it's in good shape and long enough for me to stretch out for a nap. The tables in the room, a mixture of glass, scratched wood, and what might be marble, are handy for putting drinks and pizza on, along with issues of *Entertainment Weekly* and *The Advocate* and the gay rags I never seem to get around to reading that I bring home weekly from the bars. The miniblinds shut out the light, even if they were less than twenty bucks at Home Depot.

Functional.

I move aside a stack of newspapers from the couch. "Have a seat." I head toward my kitchen with its scarred maple breakfast set and laminate almond and oak-trim cabinets. I grab a couple Stellas from the fridge and then a couple chilled mugs from the freezer. I do have *some* class! I pour the beer and then grab a couple of juice glasses for our shots of Jack.

I come back with everything on a tray and set it on the coffee table.

Randy eyes it. "You trying to get me drunk?"

"Will it help me get you into bed?"

"Not if I'm praying to the porcelain god," he answers.

"Maybe I could make my move as you bend over the toilet." I laugh, but he stares morosely forward.

I stop chuckling and sit next to him. The feel of his body beside mine, despite the tension in the room, is electric. I lean against him as I take a sip of my beer. I drink a little of the Jack and let a warm breath escape my lips. At this point in bringing someone home, I'd normally be leaning in for the first kiss. Then I'd be pulling the guy onto my lap, having him straddle me.

Smooth operator. Fast.

But Randy still is troubled. I can see it from the tightness of his shoulders, raised up near his ears, and can feel it in the way he holds himself—taut, drawn inward. He apes my actions with the beer and the whiskey, downing half the beer and all of the shot, which amounts to a triple.

He sets the bottle and the glass back on the table and eyes me. He blows out a breath before practically announcing, "My wife didn't come home last night. She was out with another guy. She's been seeing him behind my back for a while."

I'm not sure what to say because I don't know what to feel about this pronouncement. Part of me wants to wonder why he's bothered. After all, we're sitting here, on a date, and I know Randy's been out at the bars at least a couple of times. He's told me his marriage is essentially over. They're just sorting out where to take things and how to minimize how it will affect their little boy.

"Does that bother you?" It doesn't need asking, but Randy, I think, needs the nudge.

He smiles, but sadness lingers in his eyes. It's almost as though he's read my mind when he responds. "It shouldn't, should it? I mean, we're splitting up. I don't know if I need to be happy for her, but at least I shouldn't be so bothered by it."

"And how bothered are you?"

He takes another swig of beer. "It makes me sick to my stomach to think of her in bed with another guy." He finishes the beer in a long swallow and holds the empty out. "Can I have one more?"

I nod and get up to get it for him.

When I sit back down, I ask him, "What did you expect?"

He shrugs. "I don't know." He gives me a rueful smile. "Well, that's not quite true." He drinks some more beer and lets out a long sigh. "You want the truth?"

"Sure." I'm not certain where this evening is going, but it's not where I'd hoped when I was showering and shaving my balls.

"I expected her to be there for me while I sorted things out. I thought she might wait, you know, until we were split up to start dating again, to start screwing again." He hangs his head. "Selfish, I know, but it's the truth."

I'm not sure what to think or how to feel. I mean, what he's saying simply isn't fair—the expectations aren't right. Here's a woman, someone I don't even know, struggling to make sense of a marriage she thought, in good faith, was to a straight man. Is it wrong of her to seek comfort in the arms of, well, a straight man? I mean, hell, she's shook up; she's gotta be. And she's probably doubting her own sex appeal—wondering why she was the one who ended up married to a queer. And maybe being in bed with a straight dude affirms she's okay, that she's desirable.

I drink my beer, feeling like I can't voice these thoughts. It seems cruel. Besides, Randy's a smart guy. Deep down, I'm sure the same thoughts have run through his head a dozen times.

So I stay quiet.

Randy goes on. "I know. I'm being ridiculous. I was the one who set the end of our marriage in motion. I was the one who wanted to go out, meet other gay men for friendship and—" He eyes me. "—more."

"You're not being ridiculous," I say, even though I think he is. "You're grieving."

"You're wise."

"Oh, I don't know about that." I'm about to tell him we don't have to do anything tonight. He doesn't need to get drunk, as he seems to be on the road to doing. But before I can say the words, he leans forward and makes a surprising suggestion.

"Can we just go to bed? Shut this all out for a while?"

Even though an erection immediately rises in my jeans, I have enough compassion and sense to question if this is the right route to take. I take his face in my hands and kiss him—just long enough and deep enough to let him know we can do whatever he wants, especially in my bedroom. But I temper the kiss, when we at last break apart, with "Yeah, of course we can. I've been fantasizing about just that since, oh, since I first laid eyes on you back at Sidetrack last winter." I smile. "But I want you to know, we can just hold each other." I sit back, hoping he gets that there's no pressure. I know his experience with men has to be limited, and I don't want to do anything that might scare him away.

On the other hand, I'm a young, healthy, virile guy with what I suspect might be an overactive libido. I'm hungry for more than just a kiss on the lips, however nice that might be. Truth—I'd love to get down and dirty, to feel his seed spurting down my throat, to feel myself inside him and then, after a *short* rest, him inside me. I want to feel all the sweaty flesh pressed together.

God help me.

I stand and hold out my hand. He takes it and I lead him into my bedroom.

I switch on the lamp on my dresser. Anticipating we might end up here, I did put on clean sheets before making up the bed. The clothes that were on the floor of the bedroom are now tucked away on the floor of my closet. Not much improvement, but hey, I made an effort. And the room's at least presentable.

He switches off the light as I pull back the comforter. The room goes from dim to pitch-black, but after a moment, my eyes adjust, and we're in a murky darkness.

Randy undresses in the corner, where there's an old recliner I snagged from my parents' place before they donated it to the parish rummage sale. He puts his clothes on it, piece by piece, folding each one with absurd care.

I'm used to clothes being flung around the room in a blur. A contest to see who can get naked first.

But there's something about the slow and deliberate way he takes things off that moves me. In a sexual way, sure (my dick's pointed, as it should be, heavenward). But it also touches my heart. His actions reveal a scared, hungry man, and while I'd love to see the end of that fear that's become so familiar on his face, I also find it kind of poignant because so many gay guys of my generation are hyperfocused on sex and coming that they lose any possibility for true intimacy. You know, the stuff that goes beyond the physical.

Lord help me. Am I falling in love with this man?

I laugh inwardly, and a little voice sings out inside, "Too late! Too late!"

At last, he stands, hovering near the chair, his naked body as silver as the Tin Man's in the light of the moon spilling in through the window blinds. I don't quite know how to describe it, but it's like he's reluctant and seething with desire all at the same time.

He startles me when he speaks. "Aren't you gonna get undressed?"

Wow. I was so busy watching him, thinking about him, and wanting him, it hadn't even occurred to me to remove my own clothes. That's a first! "Is that what you want?"

He eyes me from across the room, making no effort to come near me, but he says in an almost strangled voice, "More than anything."

Although I don't go to the lengths of folding each piece of clothing as he did, I do take my time getting undressed. When I'm at last down to my boxer shorts, I stoop and pull them off. My dick is so hard, it slaps against my belly.

I know that, from here on out, I need to be the one making the moves. I suspect Randy would be paralyzed, his feet glued to the carpet, despite the desire I know he's feeling.

I crawl onto the bed and lie on my back. "Come on, it's chilly." I throw back the comforter a little more in a way I hope's inviting and not pushy.

After a moment, Randy moves toward the bed. He gingerly lies beside me, not close enough to touch.

I feel the weight of him on the bed. I can smell him, a little Old Spice and something deeper, animal-like, and more primal beneath the cloying commercial scent. It makes me even harder, which I wouldn't have thought possible.

My dick twitches. Precome pools on my belly.

Even though I can see his own erection in the dim light, I resist the urge to put hand or lips on it. For now.

He's lying so still. He begins talking, staring up at the ceiling. "She deserves a good man, one who finds her attractive, one who can't resist her. I know in my head I should be happy for her. And I am. In my head.

"My heart, though, is aching. With pain. With rejection." He turns to me, but still keeps his hands at his sides. He reaches up with one of them and briefly touches his chest. "This poor old heart doesn't know from gay or straight. It only knows from love. And I did love her, do love her. Just not in the way I know she deserves."

His gaze engages mine and his eyes are soulful and sad. The lids flutter. "I'm not being fair to you."

He's not. I hadn't realized it until he spoke the words. But, God, I've lost at love so many times now I sometimes think I'll take anyone who shows potential, and Randy definitely does.

And yet.

And yet.

Maybe I deserve someone who's free of the kind of baggage he's lugging around? Someone out and proud and happy? Someone who loves who he is, so he can love me, too, when he looks at me. Someone free of complications.

And yet.

And yet.

I want Randy.

It's like what he said about his "old heart" knowing only love. Despite all the red flags warning me to run like hell from this man because a liaison with him is only asking for trouble, I move toward him and wrap my arms around him.

Because love.

Chapter Thirteen

VIOLET

My mom's my best friend. There, I said it. And no, I don't think it's pathetic or sad that I find the woman who spawned me a good friend. It wasn't always this way, but I grew up, you know? We kind of became contemporaries in an odd sort of way.

It's great I have this love, this companionship.

My father's another story and one that's not relevant right now.

We sit in the kitchen of the old house in Evanston I grew up in. It's a massive, three-story affair only two blocks from Lake Michigan on Judson Avenue. It's constantly in need of painting, repairs, yard work, but my parents love this Victorian house like it's another member of the family. And maybe it is.

We all grew up here, my sister and four brothers, the classic Catholic family with kids coming one right after the other. My mom's a saint. Or maybe not, maybe more of a sinner, because perhaps if she was a little more saintly in the bedroom, she wouldn't have this enormous brood.

I'm the youngest, the baby. I'd like to say the one everyone dotes on, but that would be a lie. If you grow up in a large family, you know the baby of the family gets the least amount of real estate in the family photo albums. My older sister, Mary Pat? She's the firstborn. Go through those photo albums and you'll find pages and pages of her—first steps, first grade, first Holy Communion—all the milestones captured. By the time my parents got to me, they were obviously tuckered out from taking photographs. I take up only a couple pages in the albums, and in almost every shot, I'm in a group of brothers and sisters.

But my mom, Fran, always had a special place for me in her heart. She protected me from bullying brothers and a sister who, for the most part, ignored me. I got to do some things none of my siblings did—shopping trips downtown, lunch at the Walnut Room at Marshall Field's during the holidays, helping her make Christmas cookies.

And yet, I have never been able to bring myself to tell her about the state of my marriage. It hurts too much. I've imagined the disappointment on her face a million times, and I think, *How can I wound her like this*? She loves Randy, always has. There were times when I thought she preferred him to me!

When my father didn't want me to marry the son of a blue-collar man (welder), whom he didn't see as good enough, she fought for Randy, telling her husband that he was "a good man" and that, unlike some of the boys from Loyola Academy or our country club, whom Dad would have preferred I date, he was more trustworthy.

I knew it would break her heart to hear of our troubles and especially the truth about Randy.

But I needed her. I needed my mother, my best friend. I needed to lean on her, to embrace her maternal compassion and wisdom. I needed someone to help me sort out a situation I never thought I'd face.

We sit in the kitchen of the house. It's a big room where everyone usually ends up when there are parties or family gatherings. It's still stuck in the 1970s, with harvest-gold appliances and lots of maple. Even the refrigerator and dishwasher are covered in maple veneer.

A big pedestal table is the centerpiece of the room, and this is where we sit on a weekday afternoon in May. I've taken the day off from my job as a sales assistant at a stock brokerage house on LaSalle. Mental health day I call it, but I tell my male boss that I'm not coming in because of female troubles, and that nips any questions in the bud.

We talk a lot about little things while Mom busies herself making a fresh pot of coffee and getting a few Pepperidge Farm Milano cookies on a plate for us. Mary Pat is due to deliver her third this coming summer, and Mom's not approving of the name they have picked out for the little girl, Amber. She says it's too trendy, and she's probably right. She also doesn't approve of the fact that they know the sex of the kid already.

I remind Mom that these are Mary Pat's choices.

I hear about Denny's new job teaching English at Senn High School in Chicago, how Bobby is making great strides in his training to be a trader at the Mercantile Exchange. With a sigh, she tells me about Brad's new girlfriend and how little time this one will last...

Finally, we're seated across from each other at the table, steaming mugs of coffee in front of us. I notice Mom looks old, tired, her once vibrant red hair faded to a dull shade. The lines on her face are more noticeable, but somehow, they make her blue eyes sparkle.

Even though we've been talking about neutral stuff, family gossip, my mother has never been one to beat around the bush. She lost that capacity probably by the time she was giving birth to her second kid, if not before. She's always been unflinchingly honest.

And today is no exception. "So, what's wrong?"

I take a sip of coffee, and it burns my tongue. I pull up what I know is a shaky smile. "Does something have to be wrong for me to visit my mother?"

Ever so slightly, she rolls her eyes. "On a workday? In the middle of the week?" She pats my hand before taking a cookie off the plate. She takes a little bite and smiles. "Yes, dear, something has to be wrong. I've been a mother long enough to just know these things. Now, out with it."

I stare down at the scarred surface of the table, remembering all the meals I've eaten here, all the fighting I've done with my siblings, all the spilled milk, and the arguments. I trace a big scratch in the wood with my finger, unable to look up. I can feel the tears gathering in my eyes and the lump in my throat hardening and growing. But I don't want to cry. Not yet, anyway. I need to tell her what's happening, get out the truth before I can allow myself to be consoled.

She notices my discomfort. Even though I'm not at the moment meeting her gaze, she knows I'm on the verge of tears.

She scoots her chair a little closer and covers my hand again with her own, squeezes. "You know you can tell me anything."

"Randy and I—" I start but then have to stop because my breath is shaky, barely there. Mom squeezes again. "Randy and I are splitting up."

She snatches her hand away. It wasn't the move I'd expected.

"Tell me you're kidding."

"Tell me *you* are, Mom. I'm coming to you with something serious."

She stands and heads over to the kitchen sink. I suspect she's surprised there's nothing there for her to do, no dishes to rinse before putting in the dishwasher, no food to be destroyed in the garbage disposal. She grips the sink hard enough to whiten her knuckles and stares out the kitchen window at the circular driveway. In the center, daffodils are springing up.

She continues to peer outside, her head turned away. Her words are measured, slow, as though she wants to make sure I understand and that perhaps I'm a little slow myself. "We don't 'split up' in this family. For one, it's against the Church. For another, just name anyone else in our family who's divorced."

I can't quite believe what I'm hearing. I came here today because I thought Mom would be the one person in the world who might truly offer me meaningful support and compassion. Maybe I should have thought harder?

"Things just aren't working out," I mumble.

"And third," she continues, "What about poor Henry? He needs both his parents!"

I don't want to argue. I debate just getting up and heading home. But I can't help saying, "Henry will always have two parents who love him, no matter what."

She comes back to the table. Her face is flushed and her hands tremble. I know she's furious. "You need to patch things up." She sighs and I can see her features softening. "Sweetheart, believe me, there's nothing in a marriage that can't be fixed. All you need is some good communication and the will to make things better. I'm not saying it's easy, but it works. Trust me." At last, she locks her gaze with my own, hinting at secrets from her own marriage, secrets I don't want to know about.

The words rush out of me, words I never intended to say, knowing my family's strong Catholic and right-wing convictions. I can't help it, though. I need to make her see how hopeless this situation is.

"Mom, Randy's a homosexual."

She pauses for a moment, and her eyes widen, as though I just stood up and backhanded her across the face. And then she laughs—for a long time, until her head drops into her hands and she's shaking. I can't tell if the laughter has turned to sobbing or not.

Finally, she looks up at me and her eyes are red-rimmed, and she's a little breathless. "That's a good one, Vi. You want to try again?"

She wants the truth to be something other than it is, I know. And I can tell she already, deep down, believes me. "Mom, I wish it wasn't so. I wish I were joking."

"But you have a child."

"Yes, we do. That doesn't change who Randy is."

"Who he *is*? Honey, he isn't *gay*. If he's saying he is, it's a choice, a fantasy, some confusion on his part. He can see someone, work this out, get back to being the *man* you married."

She's running through, in a highly compressed time frame, some of my own thoughts once I knew Randy was gay—thoughts I'm now ashamed of.

I tell her being gay isn't a choice.

She waves that notion away with her hand. "Of course, it is. God made man and woman to create more of his children on this earth. You know what sin is? It's turning away from God. Randy has turned away from God." She swallows and I can see the anguish this is causing her. "He can turn back," she says quietly.

I stare down at the floor, unsure of what to say. This isn't going how I expected it to at all. I expected open arms. Sympathy. A desire to help in any way she could...

But this woman in front of me is someone I don't know. Her face is like a closed fist, and I want to recoil from it.

"He's been seeing a therapist since last winter," I tell her.

"And? Is he helping him change?"

I have to restrain myself from rolling my eyes. "No. He's helping him to accept himself. To see his worth as a person."

She's quiet for a moment, but I can practically hear the wheels turning. At last, she says, "He needs to talk to a priest, then. A priest will help him sort it out."

This time I restrain myself from snorting. A priest? He's more likely to molest my husband, but I can't tell Mom that. Ours is a family steeped in Catholicism, for better or worse.

"Mom, Randy is who he is, who he's always been. A good man. He's a great father, and I still love him."

"If those things are true, what are you doing here spitting out this filth?"

I've seldom heard my mother talk this way. I guess the topic of homosexuality has never reared its head in this family, other than my brothers and Dad making snickering jokes about the "fags."

Her close-mindedness and anger feel like a wall she's thrown up against me. I've heard it said that sometimes the only way to get out of somewhere or something is to go through it. But a brick wall? I think I'd have better luck trying to hurdle it.

And that frustrates me beyond words. I despair. And, without even thinking about it, as natural as laughter at a joke, I simply drop my face into my hands and begin to sob. I don't know where to turn for help if I can't get it from my own mother. Is there a support group for someone like me?

I could tell her I'm having an affair. That would really give her a coronary. But Steven Goode is just what his last name promises—a warm, funny man who's good in and out of the bedroom. He's nursing his own wounds from a failed marriage, but he treats me like I'm a super model or something, like he can't believe how lucky he is to be with me. He doesn't know the real reason Randy and I are splitting up. I don't know why I haven't told him. Maybe because I don't want to give the AIDS scare if he finds I'm married to a gay man. God knows I could understand how he might want to pull back from us. So, I've lied to him and told him we're already separated.

When he comes over, I hide Randy's clothes.

Mom gets up from her chair and rubs my back. "Oh, honey, is it really that bad? Is it really beyond repair?"

I sniffle and look up at her. "Yes. And yes."

She scoots her chair next to mine. Very gently, she removes my hands from her face and holds them tightly. Her touch is warm, secure, and, in spite of everything, it makes me feel safe and at home.

My lip still quivering a bit, I ask her, "What am I gonna do?"

She sighs and, finally, I can see this is hurting her too. "There's really no chance of fixing this?"

"Mom, he's *gay*. I know you don't believe it, but it's a fact. A bold, black-and-white fact. Despite what you think, he didn't choose it. Nobody chooses it. Did you 'choose' to be straight? Was there a day in, say, your adolescence, when you woke up and said to yourself, "Self, it's time to choose. Lesbian or straight? Maybe bisexual?" When I say it aloud, it sounds as absurd as it is.

But Mom just looks mystified.

"Whatever." I let a quivering breath escape. "Whatever you think is still not going to change the fact that my marriage is over."

She asks me again. "Are you sure?"

"Mom, I know. Randy has lived a lie for almost his whole life. I'm not going to be part of that lie anymore."

She leans forward so she can wrap her arms around me. She holds me close even though the position, on kitchen chairs, is awkward. "We're always here for you, honey. And for Henry."

At the mention of Henry's name, she pulls back a little, her face paling. "You don't leave Henry alone with Randy, do you?"

"Mom! Randy's gay. He's not a pedophile. He loves Henry. He would never, ever do anything to hurt our boy." I shake my head, eyeing her.

She doesn't quite look like she believes me, but she nods anyway, her lips drawn into a thin line. Leaning back, she's quiet for a long time, and I know my mother—she's working out solutions. And no other thought will do until she's found one.

After what seems like an hour but is really more likely a few minutes, she sits back, disengaging from me, and begins to speak. "You want our help?"

I nod, but am unsure what their help will entail. But I'll hear her out.

"You need to go home right now and pack a couple bags. One for you, one for Henry. You need to leave, my sweet girl. You were deceived into this marriage, and you need to get away from it. The Church will look kindly on you when they know the circumstances."

"I don't care about that."

"You should. We can get this sham annulled."

I feel a chill. I'm suddenly on a galloping horse, and the reins have slipped loose from my fingers. And yet, there's a part of me that's once again a little girl.

I want Mommy to make things all better. I listen.

"Your father has a friend who's a divorce attorney. He's very good." She nods. "He'll make sure everything will go in your favor, especially after what's happened here."

"Oh, I don't want to drag Randy's private life into this."

She stares at me and then says quietly, "You already have, my girl. You already have."

I'm full of questions, yet too overwhelmed to ask any of them. I think of my girlhood bedroom upstairs, empty these days. There are twin canopy beds. One for me and one for Henry.

Oh God, what am I about to do?

I get up. "I'll go home, get some things together."

"Good."

I move toward the kitchen door that will take me outside. I stop with my hand on the doorknob. "I'm only doing this to give myself time to think."

"Of course. We'll see you back here in time for dinner?"

I can only nod. Nausea dogs me all the way to the car.

Chapter Fourteen

RANDY

I creep around John's bedroom in the wan, grayish light that comes just before the dawn. Monday morning and I need to get to work. I dress quietly in the dim light, glad I folded my clothes carefully the night before.

Once dressed, I take a couple steps to stand near John's bed. He sleeps, undisturbed by the little noise I've made, one arm thrown over his eyes. His dark curls make a contrast against the white pillow case. The bedclothes are down around his navel, and I suck in my breath for a moment at the beauty of his broad and furry chest.

He snores lightly and it makes me smile, makes me want to get back into bed with him.

The night before was a revelation, a confirmation that I have now managed to fall into the bed I belong in—with another man. For so long, I've fantasized about doing all the things we did the night before, worried that I'd do them wrong or disappointingly.

I got no indication from John I was doing anything wrong.

Last night was perfect—the escape I needed from the mounting fears I'm having about Violet. In fact, for just a few blessed moments, I became free of all the baggage I'm sure I'll be hauling around for a while until the dust settles and Violet and I have made a kind of peace. As parents. As friends.

John stirs and his arm moves to his side. His eyelids flutter open. When he sees me, he smiles. "Hey," he says.

"Good morning," I whisper, even though I know there's no need to.

"Sneaking out?"

"You were sleeping so well, I didn't want to disturb you. I was going to leave you a note."

He turns on his side. "And what would it say?"

It probably would have said something pedestrian like "Thanks for last night. Hope we can do it again soon."

But I see an opportunity here, so I tell him, "It would have said that last night changed my life in ways you may never be aware of." I sit on the bed near him unable to resist playing with the hair on his chest. "It would have said how our time together was a validation, a confirmation I am who I'm supposed to be. No small thing. I would have told you how much I already care about you." I pause, wondering if I'm saying too much, if, like a too-soon "I love you," I will frighten him away. "I was going to ask when we could do this again."

He smiles, putting his hand over mine (the one I have on his chest). "That's sweet," he says.

My heart takes a plummet.

I move my hand away and stand up again. "Well, I should be going. I need to get home and shower and change before heading downtown." I'm wondering if he'll suggest I shower there. My mind goes into porn movie fantasy, literally steamy.

But he doesn't. "You can grab a Pop-Tart on your way out if you're hungry."

"A Pop-Tart? Seriously? I thought you were gonna get up and fix me bacon and eggs, juice and coffee."

He grins. "That doesn't happen until at least the third date."

I'm about to pounce on that, saying I'm relieved there will be a third date, but I know in my heart I've already sounded desperate enough as it is. "Are they brown-sugar cinnamon? They're my favorite."

"They are."

I lean over to kiss his forehead, feeling like a dad instead of a lover. Ick. "I'll call you or shoot you an e-mail later."

"You do that." He rolls over, away from me.

"Get some more sleep."

"I intend to. You wore me out last night."

I leave him, my smile at last restored. In the kitchen, I grab a packet of Pop-Tarts and head out to the L station on Western Avenue.

Chapter Fifteen

JOHN

As soon as the door clicks closed, I sit up. I wasn't as sleepy as I pretended. In fact, my nerves were a jumble as I lay there trying to appear relaxed and drowsy.

I get up and creep to the bedroom window, even though there's no need for stealth, and watch as Randy walks down my street. There's something sweet in this view: his innocent amble along the relatively deserted (this early in the morning) avenue.

I think how if I glanced out the window and saw him out there as a stranger, I'd be turned on. I'd be squinching my eyes together to make this hot guy come into better focus.

Instead, I just watch as he proceeds up Lincoln Avenue, headed toward the L. "Where you goin'?" I ask.

I move away from the window and plop down on my bed.

Last night was incredible. What Randy lacked in technique, he'd more than made up for with enthusiasm. I wasn't sure I could keep up, and I certainly couldn't match his four orgasms. But I figured there was a ton of pent-up sexual energy there, yearning to break free.

It was wonderful.

And concerning. Concerning because I know this was his first time with a man. And while it was most certainly *not* mine, it was my first time taking someone's virginity. The guys I've been with have all seemed to have been around the block a time or two. A time or two? Make that many, many times.

But that's okay. It's what we all do.

Except for Randy, who at age thirty-two is just beginning to discover who he is and what he wants.

And that worries me. Am I to be a learning experience? Training wheels until he learns how well he can ride on his own?

Or will he cling desperately to me, looking at me as the solution to all his troubles? His gay spirit guide and lover?

I'm ready to be someone's partner, soul mate. I don't know if I can handle or even want to be someone's mentor.

So, where does this leave us?

I'm not sure. The only thing I do know for sure is that there are enough red flags around this relationship to make it look like some kind of Russian parade.

I get up from bed and go into the kitchen to put coffee on, something I already feel guilty I didn't do when Randy was here.

But things are moving fast with us. And as much as I'm infatuated with him and as much as I want love with the right guy, something long-term, fulfilling, and *real*, I just don't know if this is something I want to or even *can* jump into. I need to protect myself—that urge is fierce.

I've lived a life where my history is full up with me throwing caution to the wind when it came to relationships. I've gone for looks, status, security, machismo, and more—all of it leading to disappointment. I've never trodden carefully because I've always thought my heart wouldn't lead me astray.

But it has, again and again.

Well, maybe it's not my heart that's led me astray.

Perhaps it was my error mistaking my heart for an organ much farther south on my anatomy. I know I tend to do that. And I regret it over and over.

While I wait for the Mr. Coffee to brew, I pull out a couple slices of bread and pop them into the toaster. Randy is not just someone I'm lusting after. I do know that much for sure, even though I've told myself the same thing about other guys a time or two before.

In retrospect, I can see those other times were wishful thinking, creating romance where there was none. With Randy, I know there's something more solid. But he has so far to go before he even realizes who he is. How does he even know what he wants at this point?

I sit at my little kitchen table with my toast and coffee and eat and drink without really tasting. My mind is too busy.

So here it is, the old war between head and heart. In the past, my heart always wins this battle.

But where has it gotten me? Sitting here alone in a cramped kitchen, eating peanut butter and grape jelly on toast and drinking bad coffee.

Maybe I need to listen to my head for a change.

Maybe I need to buy better coffee.

My head's telling me to turn tail and run—from Randy's inexperience, from his naivete. But most of all, make a hasty getaway from a guy who's still married and is jealous of his wife being with another man.

There's a whole lot that can go wrong there. I'm just setting myself up for heartbreak, right?

Chicago is filled with unattached and available guys. Why go for one who still has to go through things like moving out, a messy divorce (and you know it'll be messy), and maybe even a custody battle. Do you really want to expose yourself to a hurt spouse and maybe even the court system?

How can you be sure it would even work out in the end, anyway? He's a baby gay. Brand new. Sure, he thinks he's in love, but is he? Or has he hungered for so long for a relationship with a man, a real uniting of souls, that he's falling for the first guy who shows an interest in him?

I ask this of myself because I remember a younger John, ten years ago maybe, venturing out with a fake ID, horniness, and hope into the treacherous world of gay bar culture. I fell in love with one-night stands so many times my buddy Vince used to tease me about it, saying I was a hopeless case, that I didn't get hard-ons, I got heart-ons.

I know what it's like to be fresh out of the closet. It's scary and exciting and dangerous. All at the same time.

I push away the half-eaten toast. My coffee's gone tepid.

See, what I fear is that if I give my heart to Randy, he'll accept it gratefully. And things will be good between us.

For a while.

And then, once the dust has settled, his divorce is final, and he's no longer under the same roof with a wife, he'll look at me one day and think, "My God, I never even gave myself the chance to experience playing the field. I never got to sow some wild oats. Hell, there's a whole buffet out there, and I'm the poor sucker who only picked up one thing to put on my plate."

I think it's likely he'll think like that. It's reasonable. It has precedent. It's probably gonna happen.

If I pursue this man. If I stay a course with him.

He'll come to resent me.

And I will be right back where I started. Alone.

Why not throw my hopes and desires in with someone who's truly emotionally available and ready for a relationship? Why not give my heart to someone who's ready to settle down—and in a position to do so without clutter, baggage, wife, and kids?

Is it that hard?

I chuckle and answer myself, "Yes, it's that hard." Lord knows I've tried.

I stand up and brush the crumbs off my lap.

I go into the living room and throw myself on the couch. I pick up the phone to call Vince. He's even more of a mess than I am, but he's objective. He'll have good advice in spite of his own disastrous dating history.

We talk for a long time. I pour out my feelings, my growing fear that I'm falling for Randy, despite all the warning signs.

And, near the end of our talk, good old Vince says the words I know he'll say, the words I'm both dreading and longing to hear.

"Dump him."

Chapter Sixteen

RANDY

Walking north toward home on Ashland Avenue, I finally get what people mean when they use the phrase, "a spring in his step," because I have one in mine. I am confining myself to the spring only, although I feel like doing a little dance or maybe even singing a few bars of "Ah, Sweet Mystery of Life." If I let myself, I'd skip. Jump for joy.

It's a little after six in the evening. I had a busy day at work, which made it fly by. And now, I'm basking in the happiness that's come from being with a man, really being with one in all the good ways—physically, emotionally, intellectually—that count. I've at last experienced man-to-man intimacy, and it's making my heart sing.

I know I'm grinning like an idiot, and if anyone passes me on the street, they'll assume I'm just one of the crazies wandering around Rogers Park.

And maybe I am.

Crazy in love.

Crazy with hope that my future, something I once thought as bleak and colorless, may open up to deliver joy, contentedness, and peace.

Sometimes, being crazy is the sanest thing a guy can do.

I can still picture John in that bed. Lustful. Sleepy. Sleeping. And I can't wait to do it again, to feel his strong arms around me. To savor the sweet of his lips, his tongue. To feel him inside me, me inside him.

It's all so *good*. So right. So natural.

I use my key to open the door to the vestibule of my building. Inside, I open up our mailbox to find it empty. Violet's already been here, obviously.

As I head up the stairs to our apartment, I think how my anguish over discovering Violet has found another man is diminishing. While it still pains me, my thoughts are beginning to come around to the thought that her finding someone else is okay because that discovery is actually the key to my freedom. Rather than being jealous, I should be happy for her.

Maybe now, we can reasonably talk about it. I can tell her that I know.

And it's okay.

We've both met a man.

Now, maybe we can begin working on being parents—and friends.

I open the front door to our apartment.

I immediately notice there's something different. But it's more instinctive. It hits me within a few seconds of closing the door behind me.

I pause, still, maybe a little frightened. I expected the radio to be on, tuned to Violet's favorite station, WXRT, playing some alternative rock softly from the kitchen. I thought maybe there'd be smells—onion and garlic in butter on the stove, meat grilling.

But the place is pristine. Dust motes float in the dying rays of sunlight filtering in through our windows.

The silence is blown away by the rumble of an L train outside. I watch its passage as a silhouette behind the mini blinds at the dining room window.

"Vi?" I call out, even though I know there's no one here.

I make a tour of the apartment, hoping that she and Henry are playing a joke and I will find them hiding, say, beneath the mound of dirty clothes on our walk-in closet floor, a pile that never seems to diminish.

Until today...

The pile of clothes is gone. So are all of Violet's clothes, most of which hung on the rack opposite mine.

Heart pounding, I call out for her again and then: "Henry?"

My mind tries to calm, telling me that the two of them have taken a walk over to the little store on the corner of Jarvis and Ashland. Their prices are high, but they're super convenient when you need a jug of milk or a loaf of bread.

I sit on the bed, feeling dizzy, my heart hammering in my chest. I have trouble catching my breath. *Don't be stupid. They're not at the corner store. Her clothes are gone.*

I sit for a long time, alone and terrified of the truth that's looking me in the eye—fearless and without one ounce of sympathy. *She wouldn't just walk out on me. That's not my Violet. We'd at least talk first, right?*

My stomach churns. I fear my lunch is about to come up.

I force myself, after a time, to stand on weak knees, and make my way over to Violet's dresser. I open drawer after drawer, feeling sicker and more abandoned as I reveal each empty one.

Panting, I move quickly to Henry's room and find it, too, has been emptied out. There are still toys in the toy box, but it's half empty. There are still clothes in the closet and a few of the drawers, but curiously, they all look like ones he's outgrown.

His favorite stuffed animal, a black-and-red chimpanzee he calls Charlie, is nowhere in sight. The yellow-and-white afghan my grandmother made for him when he was born, and which he cannot sleep without to this day, is also missing in action.

Spine rigid, I stand at the window, looking out on the building's backyard, clutching a stuffed dragon in my hand so tight my knuckles whiten. But it's all I have to cling to right now, my life preserver in a world that's been turned upside down.

Throat and mouth dry, too scared to cry, I move around the apartment again, thinking there will be a note that will explain everything.

When I'm just about to give up, I find it—a folded-over piece of spiral notebook paper with my name scrawled on the outside in Violet's handwriting. She's left it taped to the freezer door.

I remove it and set it down on the little butcher's block we purchased, when we moved in, from the Ace Hardware store across from the Century Mall. I go into the pantry and see that, in her mercy, she left behind the bottle of Jack Daniels. I grab it and head into the bedroom with the bottle in one hand, her note in the other.

I take a big swig from the bottle before I open the folded-in-half paper.

At first my hand's shaking so badly, I can't focus on Violet's mix of cursive and lettering. I take another long swallow of the whiskey, blow out the liquor-heated breath, and finally calm down enough to begin reading.

Dear Randy,

You know how the song goes? The one about being cruel to be kind? That's what I'm doing now.

You've noticed we're gone. And it breaks my heart to imagine you alone there now, reading this, shocked and feeling devastated.

I know. It makes my heart hurt.

But we need to stop this.

Our marriage is a sham.

I said our marriage, not our love. Not our friendship. Not our being parents to Henry. Those things are sound, even though they need some working out in light of this new normal.

I've spoken to my family. They want to help me, and honestly, Randy, I need their support right now. I hope you understand. Your revelation last winter knocked the supports out from under me. For too long, I didn't know what to do because I was so busy thinking how I could help you.

I forgot myself.

Now that you're beginning to move slowly but surely into a world that needs to exclude Henry and me, I'm beginning to realize I have to take care of myself first. I can't be of any help to you, and certainly not to Henry, unless I do that.

My family can help me out now—emotionally, financially. They can give Henry and me a home, something I've been feeling more and more I've lost.

I don't want to whine. I don't want to shame you. You are who you are.

We'll work things out.

But for now, I need loving arms around me—ones I know will be here for me at all times, not just sometimes.

I love you, dear man. I always will.

XXOO,

Violet

I clutch the letter in my hand, wishing it were a living thing. My first impulse would be to strangle it, if it were, to blot out its existence. But after I've had time to think, I become compassionate. I know Violet needs her space, her time, and the support of someone other than me—the one who is reluctantly causing her pain.

It makes sense.

But even though I can begin to have some understanding for what she's done, I'm still confused, hurt, and full of questions. That's the thing—this letter raises more questions than it answers.

First of all, what about Henry? What's he been told about why he's been yanked from the only home he's known?

Does her being with her parents up in Evanston mean that I will, or won't, be able to see my son when I want to?

I'd like to believe that provisions will be made for me to see my son. Violet would never be so heartless. Her family, though, I'm not so sure about. The thought that they may try to take him away from me or poison his mind against me is a legitimate fear. The fact that this decision is out of my control chills me to the core and makes me sick with anxiety.

Where do I stand now with Violet? Are divorce proceedings not far behind? And if they are, will they be contentious or amicable? If it was just Violet and me, I'm certain we could effect a loving and considerate break. But with her conservative Catholic family involved? I have good reason to fear. Her parents are not only racist, homophobic, and religiously zealous, they're also powerful, wealthy people with connections.

They could make life very hard for me. I swig some more whiskey out of the bottle and then stare at it. *This won't solve anything. All this is doing is making me even more sick to my stomach.*

I get up and go back to the kitchen to replace the bottle where it was on the pantry shelf.

I walk to the back door window which overlooks the communal backyard. I imagine Henry out there with me, him chasing the big red ball he adores, him putting his hands over his ears as the L goes by just above. It's almost as if I can see him.

I have to call her. I need to know where we stand, where I stand. Her letter opened a door a bit, but not enough to reveal anything real, anything significant.

I certainly never expected her to move out while I was at work. I can't help but think it seems cowardly, even as I grope deep down within myself to be understanding and compassionate.

At her parents' house, the phone rings on and on even though I know they have an answering machine. After letting it ring at least twenty times, I hang up and call again.

And again.

And again.

Finally, the phone gets picked up after a single ring. It's my mother-in-law, and she sounds annoyed. *Well, sorry, honey, but my family and my kid are at stake here. I'm not just going to take the removal of both lying down.*

I try to rein in my anger and my terror. "Hey Fran, it's Randy. I hope you're doing okay."

Silence.

"Listen, can you put Violet on the phone? We need to talk."

More silence that stretches on for so long I wonder if she's hung up. At last, Fran says, "She's not here."

I nod, and then realize she can't see that. "But she and Henry are staying with you, right?" I don't want to give her a chance to lie, an opportunity to up the ante on my fear, so I add, "She told me so in the note she left."

Fran *tsks*, but I don't know if she's irritated with me or her daughter.

"Can I speak to my wife?"

"Now's not a good time," she replies quickly. "She's in the shower."

I roll my eyes. "Okay. I'll call back. In the meantime, could you please put Henry on?" I need to know how he's doing, what he's been told. He needs to know his daddy loves him and that this separation is *not* my idea.

"I can't do that."

"Why not?"

"He's sleeping."

"Already?" I look at the wall clock. "It's only seven o'clock. I know my son. He raises holy hell if we try to put him in bed any earlier than eight." I chuckle, but the phone's slippery in my hands from sweat.

"Look, Randy, Violet's told me, us, everything. I think it's a good idea for her to have a little time to herself, to process things, to understand what she needs to do next."

She doesn't sound reasonable, merely cold.

She goes on, "Give it a few days, okay?"

"What about my son?" I see my little dark-haired boy in my mind's eye, and I am suddenly desperate to see him.

"Henry's fine," Fran says. "Don't worry, we're spoiling him."

"When can I see him?"

"Let's talk in a few days, okay?" she says cheerily, as though she's suggesting a picnic at Lighthouse Beach.

I'm about to respond, to argue, but she's hung up.

My stomach drops. What's this going to cost me?

I sit in the living room for a long time, not drinking, not eating, not picking up the day's *Tribune*, not turning on the TV. I wait and watch as darkness overtakes what was once the home of my little family.

At last, I rouse myself and force myself to go in the bathroom, take a long, hot shower. After I dry off, I head into the bedroom, which I can use again, and lie down. But my thoughts won't let me rest, let alone sleep.

After a while, I get up and make another phone call. To John. I don't want to burden him with this, not yet. For one thing, it could very well send him screaming off into the night and away from me.

But I need some comfort. I need some support.

But when I call, it goes to *his* answering machine.

"Hey John, it's Randy," I say, trying to keep my voice light, trying to hide my despair. "Thanks again for last night." My mind goes blank, then comes up with, "Call me back when you get this, no matter what time it is. I'd love to hear your voice."

I hang up, wishing I could take back the "no matter what time it is" part, which sounds too needy.

But what's done is done.

I lay in bed the whole night through, not sleeping, waiting for the phone to ring.

It never does.

Chapter Seventeen

JOHN

I need this. This time out. This time alone. This chance to be the man I once was—carefree and unattached.

I'm at Cornelia's. It's probably the best dance bar along the Halsted strip. There's a big bar up front with the requisite giant mirror behind the bar for discreet checking guys out.

The back is where I am, clutching a bottle of Budweiser in one fist, watching the sparsely populated (it's a Wednesday night) floor, where men, some shirtless, writhe, shimmy, and shake to Grace Jones's "Slave to the Rhythm." These men are all slaves to the rhythm, and once I've had a bit more to drink, I will be too.

I need to dance, to step away from my mind for a while, to be a physical being, driven by a techno pulse that makes my hips happy, my feet irresistibly move.

I return to the front bar, ask for a shot of Jack and another beer. Both are delivered by a tattooed, buzz-cut blond who reminds me of Dolph Lundgren. He smiles and winks as he sets both down before me. "There you go, handsome."

I tip him, um, *handsomely*, because he makes me feel less alone.

I down the shot, fiery, and follow it quickly with the icy cold beer. I close my eyes for a second, imagining the alcohol coursing through me, loosening me up.

I didn't have to come out by myself tonight. I could have asked Vince, although his love affair is still burning bright, which is unusual for him. I'm both happy for him and jealous. I didn't bother calling him because lately the answer's always the same—he's busy "nesting." Am I going to lose him completely?

I could have seen if Stephen and Rory were feeling up to a night out. But I don't want a couple tonight, much as I've come to adore them. I love their easy camaraderie, their closeness, but I don't want to bear witness to it tonight.

I don't really know what I want at all, in terms of people. For once, I'm out but without a clear objective like bringing someone home or going home with someone.

I move back to watch the dancers, now gyrating to Prince and "Raspberry Beret."

I needed to escape. My answering machine is full up with messages from Randy, ranging from funny and coy to, at last, pleading.

I don't know that I can help him. I'm not sure I know how. There's a reason I never fell into the trap of conforming and marrying a woman.

Over the course of a dozen voice messages, he's poured out his whole hopeless story about how he came home to find wife and son both gone. His fears about his wife's family and how they may well make a power play to "get back" at him for deceiving their daughter and to ensure his little boy isn't "corrupted" by his new and *deviant* lifestyle. At one point, he says, tearfully, "I just know they're gonna try to take him away from me."

I feel sorry for the guy, I really do. But this is not my mess. And I can see this *is* a mess that will grow and will most likely have some staying power. Is this what I want to get in bed with?

I think not.

I just don't know if, at the moment, I want to get in bed with anyone or anything. And that's a first for me.

Which is why I find myself here, at a dance club on Wednesday night, trying hard to forget my troubles. I want to relegate to oblivion how my heart and my head are at war with each other, and I can't hear myself think because of the incoming missiles.

When an extended remix of "West End Girls" by the Pet Shop Boys comes on over the speakers, I'm compelled to move even though I'll be dancing alone. I clutch my beer and move to the center of the crowd where it won't be so noticeable that I'm shaking my booty by my lonesome.

It feels good, though, to move, to simply listen to the inner rhythm of my body, to give in to that musically fueled impulse. I let my eyes go a bit unfocused, so the other dancers become a blur of color and movement, but no one man stands out.

I feel the music, its bass line, deep down. My movements are primal and free of thought. My body simply responds.

This is where I need to be, free from thoughts, free from worry, free from concerns about my future and whether I will end up alone.

Here, deep within these movements, I find my joy.

I continue to dance until the sweat glues my shirt to my back. "No Frills Love" by Jennifer Holliday, "I Can't Wait" by Nu Shooz, "Love's Gonna Get You" by Jocelyn Brown.

Whoever's deejaying tonight knows what's in my beat-hungry heart.

I twirl, shimmy, gyrate until I'm nearly dripping with sweat, breathless, my heart pounding out its own tribal beat.

I move off the dance floor as a slower-tempo song comes on.

I need to pee.

I need another drink.

As I'm heading toward the men's room in the back, I think I see Dean out of the corner of my eye. I shake my head because he's wearing his leather harness and chaps, and this is the wrong place for that leatherman shit. But Dean certainly moves to the beat of his own drummer.

Still, I'm glad to see he's okay and still around. We haven't spoken since that night at the Belmont Rocks. I'm glad he didn't do himself any harm and glad, too, that he looks burly, fit, and healthy. The HIV in his system's apparently holding off, at least for now. Poor guy, though. He must be scared.

I pause to watch him exit through the door, figuring he'll head to one of the leather bars. I hope he won't be on his knees or bent over in the back room of one of them, carelessly and callously spreading the virus around. It makes me think of a conversation I overheard one night in one of those backroom bars. "Hey, nobody bothered to tell me they had this fucking bug, why should I? You go in a backroom and fool around, you accept that you might bring something home longer-lasting than drained nuts."

I follow Dean, forgetting for the moment my need to visit the men's room. I lose sight of him as a couple, older than the usual crowd for this place, passes between us. When my view is again clear, I look for Dean to no avail.

I move to the old oak-framed glass door and peer out into the night. Cars and pedestrians move along the avenue, but there's no sign of Dean.

I move back inside, thinking I'm probably better off for not having encountered him. The last thing I need tonight is his drama.

The door guy, seated on a high stool, grins at me. "Lose your husband?"

I laugh. "Never found him," I reply.

He laughs. He's cute, a little older, maybe late forties, with a salt-and-pepper flattop, the skinny body of a punk rocker in a, fittingly, Ramones T-shirt with the sleeves cut off, jeans, and black Chuck Taylors. He has dark eyes and a slight overbite. Freckles scattered across the bridge of his nose and cheeks.

"You looking for one?"

I shake my head, eyeing him. "You want to apply for the job?"

He narrows his eyes. "Maybe for tonight."

I pat his shoulder. "What time do you get off?"

"Twenty minutes or so, I would imagine, *after* we get to my place."

"Stranger things have happened. I'll check back with you before I leave."

I doubt I'll do that, but it seems to be the polite thing to say.

"I'll be here." He extends a hand. "Terry."

"John." I start to move away, the urge to pee reasserting itself, when I pause and turn back. "Did you see a guy in harness and chaps just go out the door?"

Terry shakes his head. "Nah, I wish. *That* I'd remember."

"Okay." A chill runs down my spine as I head toward the back of the bar.

Was it just my imagination? I could have sworn I saw him, but maybe I'm slowly going crazy. I couldn't blame myself.

After using the bathroom, I splash some water on my face and peer in the mirror. I look a hell of a lot better than I feel. I guess being on the tail end of my twenties is more of a blessing than I give it credit for.

I'm ready to dance some more.

I head back out to the dance floor. As the evening has gotten later, it's brought more and more people out, even for midweek. Cameo's "Word Up" is playing, and it's the extended remix. (I have the big twelve-inch at home, perhaps even on the turntable as we speak.) If ever a song was crafted to get people moving, it's this one. I sidle through the crowd, brushing against sweaty men on my right and on my left. It's not a bad gig!

I throw back my head and close my eyes, allowing myself to get lost in the thumping, driving beat.

When I open them, I discover I'm not alone.

A beefy blond is dancing with me, mirroring my movements a bit, and grinning as though to ask, "Is this okay?"

I move close enough to bump my hip against his to let him know it definitely *is* okay.

He's adorable. His hair is that dirty shade of blond that, when you look closely, is actually many different colors, ranging from mousy brown, to golden-like wheat, to an almost platinum shade. In his broad face, his big blue eyes are wide spaced and engaging. When he smiles, I notice, gratefully, his teeth are a little crooked, which gives him character and makes him sexier. Perfection is such a bore. He's wearing a heather-gray tank top, army-camouflage cargo shorts, and combat boots.

We continue to dance through Peter Gabriel's "Sledgehammer" and Juice's "The Rain." He's a good dancer. It's not just his moves, which are fine, but the ease he seems to have in his big body—at least six feet two and I'd guess around two hundred pounds—is obvious and points to some real confidence. He's not fat, but like a Wisconsin farm boy—*strapping,* my Gram would have called him.

At the end of "The Rain," he leans close and puts a hand on my shoulder. "Buy you a drink, handsome?"

Second time tonight I've been called handsome—and I don't think this one expects a tip. Score!

"I'd love that. Need a break, anyway."

A Janet Jackson song, "What Have You Done for Me Lately?" comes blaring out of the sound system, and it almost makes me want to turn around and head back out onto the dance floor, but my new friend is already making his way to the bar up front.

I arrive just behind him, and he turns to ask what I want.

"That's a loaded question," I say, thinking myself clever.

He raises his eyebrows. "Well, I was thinking to drink, but hey, try me. Maybe I have whatever it is you want."

Our eyes meet for a second longer than a casual glance. His are the darkest blue I think I've ever seen, and the smile on his face reaches right up to them.

"Just a Bud is fine."

He turns and orders two beers, pays, and then turns back to me. "Here you go."

I take the bottle, clink it against his, and say, "Thanks." I take a sip and then introduce myself.

"Allan," he tells me. "What brings you out on a Wednesday night?"

Before I answer, I lead him over to the side of the bar where there's a padded bench against the wall that's just been vacated. We sit.

I mull over his question. One thing I don't want to do is draw him into the drama I'm experiencing right now. Tonight was supposed to be for me—carefree, unattached me. So I tell him, "I was a little bored, honestly. And I love to dance."

He clicks his bottle against mine again. "Me too. I don't care if there's anyone dancing with me or not." He gives me a look that sends a little electric shiver down my spine. "Although I'm glad you were there—and willing."

"I get it. I don't mind being on a dance floor by myself. And it's not the same as dancing around my apartment at home, even though I do that a lot, I don't mind admitting. But even if I don't have a dance partner, per se, there's something about being part of a mass of people all moving to the same beat." I take a sip of beer. "It's almost spiritual if that doesn't sound too corny."

"It doesn't, and I'm with you, brother. There's a connection there."

I nod.

He asks, "You got a boyfriend? Husband?"

"You're very direct," I answer/don't answer.

"Hey, I find it saves me time. I know lots of dudes have open relationships or just need a little strange once in a while. That's their choice. It'll never be mine. But I always ask up front of fellas I'm interested in if they're attached or not, just in case things go somewhere."

I like this guy. His simple honesty moves me. My own lack of it, though, makes me a little ashamed. But Randy and I've made no commitment to each other. We're just exploring things. So, I'm not really lying, not *really*, when I say, "I'm single." I grin at him. "And looking."

He throws an arm over my shoulder and gives me a squeeze. "That's a relief. Do you know how hard it is these days to find a guy who isn't lugging along a whole dolly full of baggage?"

"Tell me about it." There's a part of me that does want to confide in this Allan to get his take on my infatuation with a married man, but I think if I did that, I might get some good advice back, but nothing more.

And I want something more, I suddenly realize, even if it's only a single night of oblivion.

We lean back against the wall, our thighs touching, and talk. He tells me he works for the post office and delivers mail in Ravenswood Manor, which is just across the Chicago River from my own neighborhood. He's taken a few courses at community college, but is otherwise "a plain old high school graduate" as he puts it. He loves animals and currently has two dogs and three cats in his one bedroom in Albany Park (also close to me). He reads a lot, but never fiction, and confesses to a passion for true crime and biographies. "I can tell you everything you ever want to know about John Wayne Gacy and Larry Eyler," he confesses with a wink and a grin.

"Chicago's most notorious killers of young gay men," I say. "Should I be worried about you?"

"I don't know. How young are you?"

We compare ages. He's older than I thought, thirty-eight, and assures me I'm too old to kill.

We discover we have a lot in common. And I've enjoyed talking to him so much I'm stunned when one of the bartenders calls, "Last call for alcohol. You don't have to go home, but you can't stay here."

"Is it really two o'clock?" I wonder.

He looks down at his watch. "In five minutes."

"Wow."

"Need to get home?" he asks.

I shrug. As much as I like him, I'm not sure I'm ready to open the door to anything more than this easy camaraderie we've discovered here at the bar.

"Well, I do. I have critters who are wondering where I am as we speak." He pulls out his wallet and produces a small photograph. It's one of those Sears portrait studio jobs, and it's him with his three dogs. He hands it to me and I stare down at it, heart sufficiently warmed. I figure any man who loves dogs this much and isn't afraid to show it must be a pretty good guy.

He points to each dog. First, some kind of chihuahua mix on his lap, "That's Frank. He came to me at an adoption fair at a pet store." He points to a big German shepherd seated on his right, "That's Cora. I rescued her from a shelter just before they were going to put her down. No one wanted her because she had lost a leg when she was hit by a car. She gets around just fine." He grins and I can see the love in his eyes. "And last but not least, here's Jelly. He's a mix of Pom and chow chow, I think. People tell me he looks like a little lion, and I guess that's true."

"It really is." Allan looks happy in the picture, like the smile he's wearing comes not from a suggestion from the photographer, but from a place deep inside, a place where joy lives. "You really love these guys."

"Love them? They're huge pains in the ass, each one of them." He laughs. "But yeah, I do."

"What about the cats? I don't see them."

He laughs. "You've never owned a cat, have you?"

I shake my head. "No. Why?"

"If you had, you would never have asked that question. A portrait with cats? Impossible!"

We're quiet as we rise and follow the staggering few left in the bar out the door. Terry, the bouncer, is still there at his post, and he eyes me as I pass by. He looks over at Allan, next to me, and doesn't say a word. In my head, I send him a little telepathic message: "Thanks. Maybe next time."

Out on the street, it's quiet. I assume most of the Wednesday night revelers have found, or are finding, their way home now, alone or with someone else. I imagine the love affairs that might be sparked tonight, borne of a chance encounter. I imagine too the disappointments, the dashed hopes, and the reality checks some people will experience, especially when the sun rises on another day.

Allan pauses. "You were flirting with me a lot in there."

I adopt my most innocent expression, stopping just short of batting my eyelashes. "I was?" I ask, feigning shock.

"Come on." He chuckles. "The sexual tension was thick enough to cut with a knife."

In retrospect, I realize he was right.

"You wanna come back and meet my extended family?" He leans in, looking hopeful.

Oh John, John, what are you doing? Do you really want to start something up with this guy? You have someone you're falling for, or already have. Why complicate things even more? On the other hand, Allan seems to be just the kind of man you're always imagining you want—good, simple, honest stock. And he loves animals. So he's probably nurturing and kind. And I would have sensed those things even without the pets.

Randy appears, though, in my mind's eye. Randy in my bed of all places. Randy walking north on Lincoln Avenue on his way to the L on a summer morning, eating a Pop-Tart from my pantry. Randy against the wall at Sidetrack, scared out of his wits, yet hungry. Randy leaning in for our first kiss in Stephen and Rory's darkened apartment.

Allan cocks his head. "Not a good time?"

I blow out a big sigh, wanting to both curse and kick myself. "Sorry, I have work early in the morning. Otherwise..." my voice trails off.

He nods, smiling despite the sadness in his eyes. "Okay. Maybe another time? Exchange numbers?"

"Absolutely." There's no point in completely shutting the door, is there?

Allan takes a receipt from his wallet, tears it in half and hands one of the tattered pieces of paper to me. "Good thing I have a pen in my pocket." I pull the Bic out.

"Good thing, because I certainly don't."

We take a moment to write down our names and numbers and swap.

"Maybe dinner sometime at my place? I make a mean chili."

"Yeah, that would be great. Sorry I can't make it tonight."

"It's okay. I can tell you have a lot on your mind."

"You can?" This surprises me.

"Sure. When I asked if you were single, I sensed a little hesitation, and I got an inkling." He winked. "I'm intuitive like that."

I neither confirm nor deny. "Well, hope to see you again soon, Allan." And I lean in to kiss him.

With my eyes closed, I can almost believe it's Randy.

Chapter Eighteen

RANDY

It's been two weeks since I came home to an empty apartment. Two weeks of microwaved dinners, watching whatever movies are currently playing on HBO, reading lots of pulp fiction—John D. MacDonald, Raymond Chandler, and Mickey Spillane. And day after day of getting up, going to work, coming home, and falling asleep on the couch with a book on my chest or the TV flickering out its blue-white light. Sometimes both.

But this last week, I've taken a staycation (or several mental health days in a row), trying desperately to make myself feel better, to put a little balm on my wounds.

Still, it's been two weeks of loneliness.

Two weeks of fear.

Fourteen days ago, the process server found me in the plaza outside my office building on Michigan Avenue one day at lunchtime. I don't know how he knew where I'd probably be, but when he walked up to me—all ginger-bearded and smiling, with muscles for days—I couldn't resist smiling back.

Until he handed me the divorce papers.

I hurried back to my cubicle with them, an ache in my gut, and my heart pounding so hard, I feared an attack.

Violet's lawyer is in Lake Forest, a friend of the family. I've met him before at their country club. He always seemed like a really nice man, silver-haired, and always smiling, impeccably dressed. Kindness in his blue eyes.

He-they-she are asking for alimony and child support that will take almost two-thirds of what I make (I guess the reasoning is one-third for each of us).

Somehow, I think I could manage even if I can't get a judge to pull that amount back a bit. It would mean moving out of the apartment and into a studio in a bad neighborhood or finding a roommate, but I could do it, knowing Henry was being taken care of properly.

What sends me into nightmare territory, though, is that he-they-she are asking for full custody of "the minor child." There's no provision for any kind of visitation, even supervised.

I know Violet's parents, and not Violet herself, are behind all of this. I'm sure they're funding the pricey attorney.

Still, Violet is tolerating it. I both feel for her and fear her.

I'm horrified of what they might have in store. Will my admission about being gay disqualify me from seeing my son? The thought makes me want to puke. And, if it doesn't, what kind of restrictions will I suddenly be faced with? Why do there need to be restrictions at all? I'm gay and a loving dad, not a pedophile. (Oh, I got the implication in the papers requesting full custody).

Oh Lord, why didn't I just keep the mask on? Keep my cock-sucking mouth shut and just continue to pretend I was the straight hubby and daddy? Everyone liked me better then anyway. I could even say loved me better. But, in the end, who was it they truly loved?

Is it worth all I'll lose to fully realize myself?

I left my office that afternoon after explaining to my boss I was feeling very sick (true, true, true). I told her I'd be back when I was feeling better.

AND NOW, AS I lie here on a towel on the beach at Hollywood and Sheridan, commonly known as the gay beach, I know I'll need to return to work next week. My deep tan will belie my illness, but I truly have been sick to my stomach every day.

I've talked to a lawyer, some hotshot in the Loop, recommended by Stephen and Rory. He's an older gay man who's fought against AIDS discrimination in the workplace, for one, and for all other sorts of discrimination. He's aligned with Lambda Legal and has done some divorce work with cases just like mine. We're set to meet in person next week, but he tells me he'll work hard ~~at depleting all of my savings~~ getting me the rights I deserve, the main one being the right of a father to be with the son he loves.

This past week, I've come to this beach every day. It's August in Chicago, and the weather is reliably hot and muggy, and Lake Michigan's icy waters have at last turned bearable.

It's Friday, and people are starting their weekends early. Anyone who lives here knows that winter is always just around the corner, biding its time.

Looking around, I can *almost* make myself believe that my worries are behind me. Lake Michigan is a shimmering aqua expanse, the beach is powdery, and upon it are dozens of oiled men reclining on beach towels, old sheets, and blankets. A rainbow-colored kite flies high up, dancing with a few thin strands of cloud in the electric-blue sky.

Guys fish from the long pier at the far end of the beach.

There's an oceanic tang in the air, and the sun is dazzling, golden, warming up every inch of my skin, making me sweat through the suntan lotion I've applied.

I turn over on my stomach and reach out to adjust the little radio I've brought. I'm listening to a station specializing in dance hits. The upbeat tempos are distracting and somehow manage to make me feel a little less burdened and maybe, just maybe, a tad bit closer to joy.

Until I think of what Violet is doing.

Until I think I could lose Henry.

"Hey, you mind if I move a little closer? Share your music? That's a good station!"

I turn back over and prop myself up on my elbows. There's a guy about four feet away from me, on a bright-colored, red-and-white striped beach towel. He's looking toward me, shading the view with a hand held up at eyebrow level. He's about my age, wearing a pair of Ray-Ban Wayfarers and Hawaiian-print board shorts. He's dark-haired and dark-eyed, with a bit of a pudge around his hairy middle. His smile is cute, though, with a little gap between his front teeth.

I think, only for a moment, of how I have only heard once from John in the past two weeks, and that short conversation caused me great pain, so I force it away and say, "Sure. Come closer." I grin at the guy, and he grins back.

I roll back over on my stomach, knowing exactly how provocative it looks, especially since I'm wearing red bikini Speedos.

I can hear him shifting his stuff so he can get closer. I turn my head and look at him out of partially closed eyes. He's just about aligned our two towels so close they become one.

He lies on his back, hands folded across his chest. On his back, the little gut flattens itself out. He has an impressive and dark treasure trail that disappears tantalizingly into the waistband of his shorts.

After a moment of listening to Belinda Carlisle singing "Mad About You," he asks, "You need me to rub some lotion on your back?"

I smile, but mostly to myself. I want to say, "Hey, we haven't even exchanged names yet," but I keep that to myself too. Because, see, I've had this ploy already used on me twice this week.

And, with all that's going on, this week has also been several days of asking, "What the hell?"

Without shifting much, I feel downward for the NO-AD lotion, with its piddly number-four sunscreen, and hold it out so he can grab it. "Thanks. I don't need to get burned."

He takes it from me, and in no time flat, he's kneeling next to me, kneading the lotion into my skin, lingering over the bunched muscles in my back, flirting with the base of my spine, just above the elastic waistband of my trunks. "You've got a good base," he says softly, and I notice his voice has a scratchy, velvety quality that's sexy, despite the fact it might indicate he's a smoker. "So, you probably don't really even need this, although I am more than happy to rub you down." He chuckles. "Want me to get your legs too?"

I nod.

He begins working his way from my calves up to my thighs. I can hear his breath coming a little heavier. A finger slips (accidentally?) under the elastic of my Speedos and lingers on my ass for a moment. "You must be a runner with legs like these."

"Used to be," I say, without looking at him.

At last, he's done and sits back. I look over my shoulder and can plainly see his erection making a pup tent out of his board shorts. In a moment of boldness (a trait I've acquired more and more of this week), I point at it and say, "I've got a matching one."

"Huh?" he asks and then, getting it, quickly laughs.

He throws himself down on his own stomach and now our faces are aligned. "You know, we could do something about that."

"I do know. But I don't even know your name."

"Juan. Juan Fuentes."

"Ah, so you come by your tan honestly. Unlike me. Under this bronze color, I'm fish-belly white."

He laughs at that. "I live just a couple blocks away in a high-rise on Winthrop if you wanna come by."

I let out a breath. I've been here for a couple of hours now and probably should be getting out of the sun. It's an almost totally clear day, and the heat of the rays, in the course of that time, has gone from comfortably warm to intensely hot. Lotion or no, I still can burn.

But getting out of the sun isn't the reason I'd follow him home, like some stray dog, (and, oh yes, that comparison is very deliberate).

No, I'd follow him home because I've learned fast how sex with a stranger can blank my mind with oblivion. For the intensity of those skin-to-skin moments, none of my problems exist—no upcoming custody fight, no getting ditched by John, whom I thought I was falling in love with, no worries that I'll be a pariah to the friends and family I still haven't come out to.

I've learned that lesson almost every day this week, right here on this very beach. Well, not right *on* the beach, but that's where propositions get made. I'm discovering fast how easy it is to find sex if you're a young gay man in Chicago.

The trick (if you'll pardon the pun) is finding love.

That sucker is elusive. I'm learning that fast too.

Do I want one more encounter in some stranger's apartment? Do I want to leave, yet again, balls drained but feeling vaguely dissatisfied? None of the guys I've left the beach with have compared to that one night with John. And there have been a couple of real hotties! One was a bodybuilder. Another did some modeling and, I suspect, porn. Sex with all four of the guys I've been with this week has been satisfying, but only in the way a hamburger or a slice of pepperoni pizza is satisfying when you're famished.

After, I feel ill-nourished and wanting more.

So, do I want to go home with Juan?

I don't know. I dodge the question by standing up and announcing, "I'm gonna take a quick dip." I smile, and so he won't lose hope, add, "First."

I dash through the sand and into the water. Despite having said that it's warmer, the water is still bracingly cold, just a couple degrees above bearable. I wade out into the surf, gasping a little as the waves rolling in hit the dry parts of my anatomy. The shallows extend for quite a way out, and it's not until I'm pretty far from shore that I allow myself to dive in.

Submerged, I open my eyes to a darkened world, blue-green. The sun's rays are diffuse through the water, moving as another big wave crashes over my head. Below me, pebbles and sand shift with the ebb and flow of the waves. A school of small fish swim by.

I hold my breath until my lungs hurt, kicking out farther and farther. When I at last allow myself to push up again to the surface, I turn to see the beach, far off in the distance. I think, for just a moment, of heading farther out into the deep, toward Michigan, swimming and going under until I can't do it anymore. It seems romantic, now that my body has accustomed itself to the water's chill, to imagine myself just disappearing in this aqua expanse, sinking down not only into the lake, but into oblivion.

Free. I'd be free.

I turn and head back, knowing that such an idea is, in reality, neither romantic nor realistic. Death by drowning, I know, wouldn't be a pleasant experience. It wouldn't be like falling asleep in a wave's embrace. My own body and lungs would struggle mightily against my betrayal. There would be panic and pain.

Ah shit, why do I even allow myself these thoughts? *Because, my dear, you're feeling alone, isolated, and that no one in this world loves you—the real you, the one who's hidden behind a mask for most of your life.*

As I wade out of the water, I think of my last conversation with John, hoping the whole time he was telling me he couldn't see me anymore that he'd pause, think about what he was saying, and reverse his decision.

But he didn't.

And, in the end, he used a metaphor that's apt for me right now as I wade out of the water, the brilliant sunshine already drying and heating my skin.

He said, "I just can't handle being with you. You're a great guy. But I know, I just know, that you're also drowning in a way, and reaching out to me is the same as a drowning man reaching out for the handiest thing to keep himself afloat, to keep himself alive."

I argue with him, telling him he's wrong (but maybe he isn't), but his mind was made up.

On the beach, I see Juan sitting up, smiling and waving at me.

Yes sir, I'll go home with you.

LATER, AS I head north on Winthrop Avenue toward the L stop at Granville, I think how my time with Juan couldn't have been more disastrous.

I started having misgivings as soon as I entered his darkened studio apartment. Because of the contrast of the sun to the basement interior, I was almost blinded when we walked in the door. Gradually, I could make out a diffuse light coming in from a narrow window, little more than a slit, high up on one wall. When he said he lived in a high-rise, I was expecting panoramic views of the lake and the skyline.

Not this hole.

It smelled bad too. Like garbage left too long in the kitchen, something organic, yet rotten. Over all of this, not masking, but making things worse, was the stale smell of cigarette smoke.

As my eyes adjusted, I could make out how tiny the place was, with a door leading to what I guessed would be a bathroom, a kitchenette along one wall and, dominating the space, a messy queen-size bed, its coverings half on the bed and half on the floor. The sheets were coming off the bottom end, revealing the striped mattress ticking underneath.

Juan gave me a weak smile. I suspect he could tell I was a little put off by the squalor he was living in. "Sorry. I wasn't sure I'd be bringing someone back from the beach." Halfheartedly, he tightened the sheets on the bed and pulled up the comforter from the floor, laying it across the bottom.

"You like porn?" he asked, eyes brightening with hope.

"I guess. Who doesn't?"

He squatted down in front of a small, wood-laminate entertainment center and popped in a videocassette. In minutes, the screen above the VCR came alive with a crowd of lined-up men, sucking and fucking.

He grinned. "*LA Tool and Die*—it's one of my favorites."

"Hot," I said without much enthusiasm, eyeing the screen, then looking back at him.

He crawled over to the coffee table at the foot of the bed and opened a drawer. He took out a small vial and spilled some white powder onto its surface. Using a credit card he'd pulled from his wallet, he separated the powder into lines. He got up and went into the kitchen and returned with a drinking straw cut in half. He held it out to me. "You party, right?"

He slid out of his trunks, standing naked before me.

He was hard.

I was not.

I shook my head. "Not really. What is that?"

He looked at me like I was an idiot, a child. "It's coke, man." He waved the straw toward me. "You've done it before, yeah?"

I shook my head.

He kept holding the straw out to me. "Where have *you* been?" He laughed. "Don't be so uptight. Do a couple lines. It'll make the sex incredible."

When I didn't take the straw from his hand, he squatted at the table's edge and quickly snorted up three lines. He rubbed some of the powder left over from them on his gums. "I don't care if you do it or not, but, really, you'll have a blast. Sex like you couldn't imagine. Maybe I can even call a couple of my buddies over later."

Despite the hardcore porn and Juan's naked body, close enough to touch, I felt no desire whatsoever. All I could think of was Henry, imagining him seeing his daddy in this filthy place with someone he didn't know two hours ago. Doing drugs. Taking part, perhaps, in a gangbang.

I felt ill.

I edged backward, toward the door. "Uh, sorry, man. This isn't for me. Not today," I said and thought, *Not ever.*

He snorted another line and crawled naked onto the bed. Staring at the screen, he lit up a cigarette and began tugging at himself. "Suit yourself. You still wanna stay, though, right?"

I backed up until I could feel his front door at my back. I reached behind me to grasp the doorknob. I turned it slightly. "I don't think so. Sorry. I think you and I like different stuff."

"Oh come on, sit down, do some blow, watch a little of this flick. It's amazing."

"No."

I opened the door and felt like I could breathe again.

"Fag," he said, not taking his eyes off the screen.

NOW, AS I climb the stairs to the L platform, I wonder how calling me a fag made sense given the situation we'd found ourselves in.

When the train pulls up, I board and collapse gratefully into an empty seat. Across the aisle from me, once the train is in motion, a bleached blond guy, with what looks like a big purple birthmark, eyes me and smiles provocatively.

I turn away, staring out the window, watching the backs of apartment buildings as the train picks up speed.

Once I get home, I'm grateful to be at my front door. I feel like I did as a kid in a game of tag—I've reached home base.

I'm glad I've discovered the beach a few L stops south, but thinking maybe I should be more cautious about who I let take me home.

Or maybe I shouldn't go home with guys from the beach at all.

Once I open the door, I can tell something's different. There's an indescribable energy in the air. I can't quite put my finger on what it is, but it makes me feel violated.

I wander through the rooms, which doesn't take long. One of the things that drew Violet and me to this place was its "vintage charm." The ad for the apartment used just those words. High ceilings, crown moldings, original hardwood floors, a fireplace, and lots and lots of built-in cabinets. The sunlight streaming in through the big windows was magical.

It's the built-in cabinet in the pantry that clues me in on why something feels amiss. The shelves behind the glass doors are empty. They weren't that way when I headed out to the beach.

On the shelves were all of the good Lennox china we got as wedding gifts. I eye the shelves, pristine, empty, as though the plates, bowls, cups, and saucers had never been there in the first place.

I stoop a little to open the drawer beneath the shelving. Yup, all the silver flatware we also received as wedding presents is gone.

Getting a clue, I walk around the apartment once more. In the dining room is a little oak trolley, upon which, once upon a time, sat our silver service. We never used it, but it was a legacy from Violet's grandmother, hence its place of honor in our dining room.

The silver service is gone too.

So is the oil painting of irises that once hung over our couch. The wall behind it is lighter, highlighting the loss.

I plop down on the couch. I don't care about any of these things. And I don't believe I've been robbed—the doors and windows are all still locked. Besides, the choice of items to steal are way too specific for a burglar, who would have taken stuff like, I don't know, the stack of credit cards I left on my nightstand before heading out.

"Why, Violet?" I wonder aloud to the sunbeams radiating in through our big living room windows. "Did you think I would fight you for this *stuff*?" I shake my head, knowing that it couldn't have been Violet's idea to come in and highjack our wedding presents. No, I'm certain, with no one even telling me, that idea came straight from her mother, Fran.

I can see this, as much as being served the divorce papers, as a declaration of war.

This doesn't have to be a battle.

I sit and absorb this betrayal for a while. "Why didn't you just *talk* to me, Vi? I would have *given* you anything you wanted. You didn't need to sneak in behind my back, for God's sake."

I get up and move to the phone to try to call her once more.

Of course, the phone rings and rings at her parents' house, at last ending up with the answering machine and its automated message. It's the same old story. I haven't spoken to Violet since she moved out. It's the same story at her job, where they've obviously been put on alert—Vi is always in a meeting.

I hang up without a message. Nothing I would say would do much good, if they even allowed Violet to hear it.

My next call is to the attorney downtown.

I have a proposal for him, something simple, but I hope he can make it happen.

Chapter Nineteen

JOHN

Finally, Vince has cleared an evening with Arvin, his not-so-new beloved to come out with me. It's been so long since I've seen the guy I thought was my best friend that I asked him to come out early and to do something different than what we usually do, which is go bar-hopping.

We're seated at a table in the window of Las Mananitas on Halsted. Over jumbo, too-strong margaritas and chips and salsa, we watch the parade of boys go by, heading out to the bars. I was one of them once, now I feel I'm looking at them in a way that's once removed.

"So you followed my advice to dump the guy?" Vince drains his glass and signals our waitress for another round of margaritas. I will need to be wheeled home in a wheelbarrow.

"Yeah." I pop a chip into my mouth and look into his eyes. There's concern there, and I know what he told me to do was the right thing, but these last two weeks have been miserable. I've picked up the phone to call Randy a dozen times. Only a supreme effort of will makes me put the receiver back in its cradle before he, or his machine, picks up. "I did."

"And how did he take it?"

I wait until the waitress clears away our glasses and sets down two more margaritas.

"We should probably order some food to soak up some of this tequila," I say before the waitress leaves the table. Vince orders the chicken quesadillas and I the carne asada. We've both been here so many times we don't even need to look at a menu.

After she leaves, I answer. "He took it as you might expect."

"Heartbroken?"

"Devastated. Wouldn't you be?" I smile, but there's no heart behind it. It may seem to Vince that I'm joking, but in all kidding, there's always at least a little seriousness. Randy was beyond hurt when we had a brief phone conversation, (and yeah, bad me for breaking up over the phone even if breaking up might be too sober a term for the early days we were in).

"Well, he'll be okay," Vince tells me. "I mean, you guys hardly even dated."

I want to ask how he knows Randy will be okay—he's never even met the guy.

"He needs to get his own head on—you should pardon the expression—*straight* before he has a relationship. And you need to have yours examined before you launch into another infatuation with another married or otherwise emotionally unavailable man. It's a pattern for you, you know. You'll never win if you're always betting on losers."

He's right, of course. Still, there's a hollowness at my core that's been there since that awful phone call. I'm ashamed to say that the call only happened because I, in a moment of weakness, picked up the phone instead of letting the machine get it. My sad modus operandi has always been to just stop calling or returning calls, and becoming a ghost.

No message, I told myself, *is* a message. Why can't people ever get that?

Still, when I told Randy I couldn't be his training wheels as he ventures into the gay world, I felt like someone forcing himself to choke down a big bowl of unseasoned spinach—you know it's good for you, but it tastes like hell.

Vince eyes me once our food arrives, his head cocked.

"What?" I ask, even though I know the answer. I dig into my food.

"You. You're trying to make me believe you don't care when it's obvious you do. You joke about Randy being heartbroken, but I think you're the one. You should see yourself through my eyes."

"I don't want to," I snap. What Vince sees is some lovelorn sad sack. Pathetic.

We finish our meal in near silence. When we do talk, it's about trivial stuff—the heat wave we're having and how it's causing brownouts and blackouts all over the city, the new bars that have opened up in the Andersonville neighborhood, our respective jobs—how I save lives and he buries the ones who can't be saved.

We settle up the bill. "Thanks for coming out tonight."

"It was good to see you."

"You wanna go for a drink?" I ask. "It's comedy night at Sidetrack."

He sighs before standing. When he does, he says, "Ah, I should probably just get home."

"Home? You haven't moved in together, have you?"

He waits a beat before answering, maybe out of consideration for my lovelorn feelings. "Yeah. I wanted to tell you. Just waiting for the right moment."

He doesn't say why he didn't, but I can guess it's because I poured out my heart over dinner how miserable I was over nipping this "thing" with Randy in the bud, despite feeling it was the right thing to do. But I hate that my friend doesn't want to share his good news with me because he's afraid it'll make me feel bad.

Is the right thing to do *always* the right thing to do? I wonder.

"Arvin and I want to have you over for dinner soon. You and a date. You *are* dating, seeing people, right?"

"Sure." The truth is, I haven't been with anyone other than Mr. Thumb and his four sons in weeks. "That would be really nice. You sure you don't want to come out for a quick one?"

Vince shakes his head. "Sweetie, if I have another, I'll be under the table. Or under some guy, and I'm trying real hard to make this relationship work. Stay true."

We head out into the night. It got dark while we were inside, but the shadows brought no relief. The temperature must still be near a hundred with the humidity about the same. It feels like someone threw a wet blanket over me when I moved from the refrigerated restaurant to now-tropical Halsted.

We kiss on the street, on the lips—a quick peck. Buddies. It's sad that, even here in the gay epicenter of this metropolis, we have to look around guiltily after exchanging a simple gesture of affection.

Vince says, "Go on. Go to Sidetrack. Get drunk. Get laid."

I nod.

He punches me in the shoulder. "Cheer *up*, buddy! I've never seen you like this."

"I've never been like this." And it's true. I haven't. I blow out a breath of air. "Go on home, now. Give that man of yours a kiss from me." I turn back toward the restaurant. "I'm gonna grab a *Gay Chicago*."

We hug once more, and I duck back inside to grab the paper.

When I come back out, paper in hand, I decide not to go to Sidetrack or any other bar. For one, I'm comfortably "happy" from the tequila I've just had. One more drink though and I'll be stinkin' drunk. Fine line, you know. For another, I'm no longer in the mood. I wish I could be. I wish I could go to a bar with a backroom and just get off like I once did without thinking about it, without worrying about silly things like, oh, jeopardizing my life.

This last thought makes me think of Dean Carvello. I wonder once more how he's doing. I recall seeing him on my last night out and hope he's found a measure of happiness, I really do. Despite his histrionics and the brush with stalking, I once cared about him and thought we had a future together.

Despite not wanting to head out for more drinks, I don't want to go home yet, either.

I walk down Halsted and turn on Belmont, head west to the Dunkin' Donuts at Clark. Hey, at least I can have a glazed doughnut and watch the parade of weirdos always hanging out at that corner. They're often funny, sometimes scary, never boring. It's cheap entertainment.

I go in and order a coffee, a glazed doughnut, *and* an apple fritter because I just don't give a damn how fat I'll get. Sometimes sugar and carbs are the perfect comfort food.

I sit down with my treats at a window table and open the *Gay Chicago*. I begin turning pages, looking at pictures of people out having fun at the bars—a cute couple celebrating their first anniversary, several different drag queens performing around town, a fundraiser for an AIDS charity, the dance floor at Roscoe's.

It doesn't take me long to find the obituaries. I've watched those pages grow and grow during the last few years as AIDS claims the lives of more and more of my brothers. It gives me a chill every time.

I'm about to skip over the section when I see someone I know.

I lose my appetite all at once.

I stare down at the memorial, hoping my eyes deceived me. But no, it's there in black and white with a formal studio picture. Dean Corvello. I close my eyes as a jolt passes through me. When my breath returns, I read over the details—age, occupation, survivors, school information—and how Dean passed away after a "short illness."

My heart feels like it's moved up into my throat. My breath comes a little quicker. If I don't repress the bile rising up, I could lose my dinner. Sweat beads pop out on my forehead.

I'm pretty sure this is what a panic attack feels like. I've never had one myself, but I've seen quite a few in my work. I don't want to be sick, don't want to have to breathe into a paper bag right here out in public.

But I'm wrecked.

Dean Corvello is *dead*? I thought, when we talked on the Belmont Rocks that night he'd just found out, that he was going to be okay. After all, he'd just found out. It could be a long time before an opportunistic infection made him sick, maybe even longer before something as extreme as death.

Our encounter was only a short time ago. Mere weeks.

But being diagnosed and getting sick could happen really quickly. The hateful virus could live in one's system silently for a long time, doing quiet damage while the host is none the wiser. I'd seen enough instances to know how insidiously things worked when it came to HIV.

But still? Dean?

I'd just seen him! I remember trying to catch up to him as he left Roscoe's in his harness and chaps, looking fit as a fiddle.

I glance down again at the obit. Look closely at the date when he passed away at St. Joseph's Hospital. I shake my head.

It can't be.

But it is.

He passed away on exactly the same night that I saw him. I close my eyes to ward off the dizziness.

It couldn't have been him. It's that simple. It must have been someone who looked like him.

But it was...

No, no. It's just not possible.

It may not be possible, but you know what you saw. It wasn't a mistake.

Whatever. What does it mean?

I place my head down on the plastic table.

I feel a hand on my shoulder. I suck in a trembling breath and force myself to look up. A young black woman in the Dunkin' Donuts uniform stands over me, concern plain in her dark-brown eyes.

"Sir? You okay?"

I nod because I don't feel composed enough yet to put thought, tongue, and lips together to form words.

"Can I bring you some water or something?"

Finally, "No. It's okay. I just found out a friend of mine passed away. I didn't know. It was a shock."

She glances down at the paper, open on the table.

"AIDS?" she asks.

I nod again. "I think so." I wonder how she knows. She didn't have time to read the obituary. And even if she had, all she would have seen was short illness, not the twentieth century plague.

She wanders away. She whispers something I barely hear that sounds like "He's okay." I close the *Gay Chicago* and stand. I take my uneaten food to the garbage can and throw it away. Right now, it feels as though I'll never want to eat again.

As I near the exit, I turn to thank the young woman for her concern, but the only one behind the counter is an older man with a bald pate and wire-rim round glasses. He's lazily wiping the counter with a rag. He doesn't look up.

I feel a chill that's not dissipated as I head out into the hot and humid night.

WHEN I GET home, I try to sleep. I succeed, surprisingly, right away, but the dream wakes me. And when my eyes fly open, with my heart hammering out a tribal beat, I recoil at how my sweat has soaked my sheets and pillowcase.

Night sweats?

I'd dreamed of Dean. It was that same night I'd seen him—or thought I'd seen him—at Roscoe's. In the dream, though, I did manage to catch up to him just outside the bar's front door.

"Hey Dean!" I call. He doesn't turn, doesn't give me any indication he's heard me even though I'm right behind him. I call out a couple more times, but all I see is the back of him as he strides quickly away. His broad shoulders defined by the leather-studded harness and the way the chaps highlight his ass in tight, faded denim draw my eye, making me a little breathless with desire.

I follow him east, down shaded streets alive with dancing night shadows. Silhouetted leaves on the pavement move with the wind. It's eerily quiet—even the sound of my footfalls is muffled, barely there. It's like one of those nights when I've stayed out until a bar with a four a.m. license closes, and I'm looking for a taxi.

All at once, we're at the lakefront. The sound of the waves rushes in, and I look out to see a full moon reflected on the water. Its silver glow rises and falls as the lake moves to its own rhythms. I watch Dean cross a broad expanse of grass, heading toward the rocks.

"Dean! Please wait up. I'd heard you died. But that was a mistake, huh?"

He mounts the boulders at the edge of the black water and stands for a moment, looking out. He raises his arms to something—the night? The moon? God?

When he turns, I gasp. It's not Dean's face, but Randy's. His gaze, even in this silvery light, connects with my own.

I rush toward him.

He falls backward, disappearing from my view.

There's no splash, but I know.

I know.

What I see when I get to the top of the rocks is empty water, restless, throwing itself with fury against the boulders.

I get up from bed. The sweaty sheets are clammy against my skin. Gross. I pad out to my kitchen and draw a glass of water from the tap and then gulp it down. I refill it and glance up at the clock mounted on the soffit above the sink. It's just past two a.m.

I know what I need to do.

I take my glass to the living room and sit on the couch. Very deliberately, and ignoring the logical protests my mind is shouting at me, I dial Randy's number. I know it's too late.

I also know it's never too late.

He picks up after a couple of rings.

The sound of his voice causes a little catch in my breath, maybe even a skipped heartbeat.

"Randy?"

"Yeah?"

"It's John."

All I get is silence, and I'm afraid he'll hang up, so I simply say, "I was wrong. I miss you. And I need to see you." I think my statement will be met with scorn, laughter, or indifference.

But Randy merely says, "There's a solution for that, you know."

Can it be? Could it be?

"What's that?"

"Come over."

Normal folks would complain it's far too late. But that lateness, that stillness that makes it seem like the whole world's asleep is what makes it so natural for me to say, "I'll be right over."

We disconnect and I hurry to get ready.

As I head out the door, I think that I'm not headed for the Rogers Park neighborhood, but for the rest of my life.

Chapter Twenty

RANDY

I wait alone in the conference room. It's hard not to be nervous, even though I requested this meeting. I feel like so much rides on the next hour or so. My life, my family, and my love are all on the line.

I try to distract myself by taking in the plush furnishings of my attorney's Michigan Avenue office—all that cherrywood and brass, the sedate oil paintings on the eggshell-colored walls. The windows look out on the lake and Navy Pier. The Tribune Tower's gothic conceits.

It's the tail end of summer, and the sun causes the water to sparkle. Someone has cast diamonds on its surface. Cumulus clouds add a little drama to the neon blue of the sky.

The door creaks open, startling me.

Violet stands poised in the open doorway as though debating whether to come inside or not. I haven't seen her since she slipped out of our apartment several weeks ago, and she seems changed. She might be a little thinner. Her makeup has been applied carefully, and there's more of it than she usually wears. Despite this, she looks tired, and her eyes project weariness as well as wariness.

I smile and hope it calms her. "Come on in. I won't bite."

She enters and closes the door behind her. Her footfalls are muted on the plush beige carpet. She sits in one of the leather chairs across the big table from me. Finally, she meets my gaze and gives me a little smile.

"I'm here," she says.

I remind myself to try not to be disappointed that she's not friendlier, that her attitude toward me is chilly. Maybe this is a great concession on her part. I don't know.

"And I appreciate it, Violet." I try to gather my thoughts, my wits, my words. I attempt to stem the anxiety that's making my stomach hurt and my palms sweat. "I asked that we have this meeting so we could just talk—you and me, alone. No lawyers, no parents, no psychologists trying to tell us who we are. Just us. The way we once were. Do you think we can talk?"

Violet crosses her arms and looks out the window. "It's beautiful out there."

I nod. "How's Henry?"

"He's good. He's really getting into his little Nintendo gadget." She smiles and, for a moment, her face lights up.

"I miss him." I hope she'll come back with "He misses you," but if she has anything to report on that score, she's keeping it to herself.

I hold it back—asking her if he ever asks about me. If he doesn't, I don't want to know.

I haven't been allowed to see my son in far too long. I wonder if this would be a problem if I were a straight man, but not too much. I know. It's my shame. My heartache. My little boy could be kept from me, and the world would condone it.

I've always been a loving dad.

But this meeting that I asked my lawyer to set up is not for the airing of grievances. No, this meeting is for the purpose of getting Violet and me alone together for a little while, simply to talk and to see if the two of us can make our way out of this mess without having to resort to more depositions, psychological evaluations, and eventually, a hearing.

I reach down to the floor and slide a Toys"R"Us bag across the table. "Those are some games for Henry's Game Boy. The receipt's in there so he can exchange them if he already has them. Or if he wants something I didn't know about."

The room grows quiet. The air-conditioning hums. I wonder if the chill from it is making me shiver—or is it from something simpler and more complicated—my terror.

"What do you want from me?" Violet asks. She uncrosses her arms and leans forward.

"I just want to see if we can work something out, see if we can maybe come to some terms on joint custody."

"Joint custody?" Violet shakes her head. "It's not gonna happen. My parents would never allow it."

Your parents? Your parents? What about you?

Be calm. Don't shout. Don't cry. Just talk. "Why? Because I'm gay? Vi, you know I'm a good dad, a good person. You know I'd never harm Henry. I want only the best for him."

"I do too," she says, her voice trembling a little.

"Then why are you keeping him from me?" I don't want to bring it up, the night I went up to Evanston with a police escort, so I could see my son. I'll never forget the flashing lights of the police car, the way the crew-cut blond officer seemed unwilling to help me, seemed almost amused by my existence. He was relieved when my mother-in-law told them that Henry was not in the house.

The officer wouldn't listen to me when I argued that Fran was lying.

The worst horror was when he finally drove away, his flashing blue lights extinguished. Fran had already gone back inside, incensed that I would have the nerve to bring the cops to their suburban home.

As I got back in my car, the tears now coming, I looked to an upper-story window. Henry appeared there, in his pj's, his cowlick sticking up. He pressed a hand to the glass. I raised my own hand to wave, but I'm not sure he saw because Fran pulled him away from the window and drew the curtains.

"I'm just keeping him away until we can get things worked out. Terms, you know?" Violet's eyes are glassy with tears, and I know this is hurting her too.

So why is she toeing the line?

I shrug. "I don't really. I don't know, Vi. We were a family. We loved one another. I still love both of you. That's why I asked if we could meet today, to see if we could go back to being Vi and Randy and just settle things. All I want is to be able to see Henry. I don't care about stuff—material things. You can have it all." I know my lawyer would be clapping a hand over my mouth if he were in the room with me. "I'm happy to do whatever we need to about money and child support. I'm not gonna fight you on any of that stuff."

"Really?"

"Yes, really." I get up and move to the other side of the table so I can sit next to her. I try to take one of her hands in my own and quickly learn what a mistake that is when she snatches it away, drawing it back close to her body.

"Don't," she says softly.

"Violet. Why? Can't we just make some decisions on Henry?" I'd love joint custody, but I know that, at this point, I'm asking for too much. My own sense of shame and self-loathing, I realize, logically prevents me from pressing for more. So, I offer what I think is pathetic, but hope is acceptable enough. "How about this? One night a week for dinner and a sleepover. And then one day out of the weekend? That's not too much, is it?"

She stares at me for a long time. I watch as a couple of tears rise up and dribble down her cheek. She wipes them away with the palm of her hand, seemingly angry at the betrayal of her very own eyes.

"My parents have bought Henry and me a condo in Evanston up near the Northwestern campus. It's nice. Henry'll have his own room that looks out on the courtyard. It even has an en suite bath."

"Why are you telling me this?"

"My parents are paying for him to go to St. Simon's in the fall."

"A Catholic school? Really, Vi? I thought we agreed we wanted him to go to public school, so he could meet different kinds of people."

"It's a good school," she says. "We don't have to pay a dime."

She crosses her arms and swivels the chair to look out the window again. "I know you hate them, but they've been a real help to Henry and me."

I don't know what to say. I don't know what to do. I get what's between the lines here. My soon-to-be-ex-wife has caved, has been bought. She will sell our son in exchange for security.

I feel like I'm going to be sick. "Please, Violet, I'm begging you. Don't let them do this. We don't have to go to court and bankrupt ourselves." I doubt Violet has any worries about bankruptcy, even though I do, given her parents' deep pockets. "Just let me see Henry. One day a week," I plead.

She's on shaky legs as she stands. "We close on the condo next week."

"What? How's that relevant?"

She grabs the Toys"R"Us bag and then moves toward the closed door. With her hand on the knob, she says, "I'm sorry, Randy. I really am. I just need to do what's best for our son." She sniffs. "And for me."

"In what world is keeping a boy from his father what's *best*?" I cry out, losing my control. "I love him, Vi!"

She starts out of the room, and I push back the chair to get up and follow.

She must hear me because she pauses in the doorway and turns back. Her eyes are wounded. It's almost as though I can sense a desire on her part to reach out to me. She swallows. "Randy. Do you regret any of this? What you've done? The lies? The pain you've caused?"

I'm so shocked, I plop back down in my chair. Part of me wants to take on the pain she's sending my way. That part, still not dead despite therapy and my own self-actualization, hasn't flatlined yet. "Regrets?" I shake my head. "No, Vi. How can I have regrets when I didn't choose who I am? I could die, smothered under a mask, or I could lay down my sword and my shield and stop fighting—with myself. I can choose to live an honest life as my authentic self."

Vi stands frozen, her lower lip trembling. "An *honest* life?" she scoffs.

I ignore her and go on. "And I *don't* regret our marriage...and not just because Henry came out of it.

That's a wonderful plus. But we had good years together, didn't we? We were happy. It wasn't just me. I'm sorry if it took me so long to accept who I am, but it doesn't mean I didn't love you. I did. I do. And I believe I'll continue to, no matter what.

"Regrets. Huh-uh, no. Do you?"

She closes her eyes for a minute, and I wonder what she'll say.

But she says nothing. She simply turns and walks away.

I jump up and follow her down the long hallway toward the lobby with its chrome and leather. I watch her pace quicken, the sway of her hips beneath the long floral patterned skirt she's wearing.

We get to the lobby.

And Henry's there with his grandma. My heart rises and I can't help myself. "Henry!" I cry, joy coursing through me like a drug. I drop to my knees right there in front of the half dozen or so strangers seated in the lobby.

Fran wouldn't dare hold him back in front of these people, would she? And I know Violet wouldn't, couldn't. Despite everything, I still cling to the knowledge that Violet has a heart.

My boy runs to me. My boy is in my arms. I squeeze him to me tightly, my breath gone, feeling only a huge swell of love that surrounds the two of us in a cocoon of warmth. I can't believe how small he feels and, paradoxically, how big he feels in my arms. Solid. Real.

I hold him for a time, and then we pull back and look into each other's eyes. Henry's smiling.

"I've missed you so much, son."

"Did you, Daddy?" Henry sniffs and I can tell he's trying not to cry. "Grandma and Grandpa said you didn't want to see me. They said you had a new life."

I shake my head. "Henry. That's not true. I miss you every day." I think about telling him about all the calls I've made to the house, my trip in the night with the cops, the letters I've written—all the futile efforts I've made to try to see him, if only for a moment. All thwarted by people whom I hope believe they're doing the right thing, that they're doing what's best for the child. But I don't tell him any of that stuff. He's just a little guy, and he loves his mom and his grandparents. They're his family, too, however much they want to thwart my relationship with him.

Bottom line, I know Henry can use as much love in his life as possible, so I'll just try to focus on the positive.

"Listen, I always want to see you. I always want you to be in my life. Every day. You're my little boy. I love you. Don't let anyone tell you any different. Grandma and Grandpa love you, but they're mixed up—they got it wrong."

I look up to see Fran and Violet standing above us. Fran's lips are compressed into a thin line, and I can see she's holding back her anger. I try to believe that, just like I am, she's looking out for her baby. Right or wrong, she views me as a bringer of pain, a threat. Still, it's hard not to throw that hate and rage right back in her face.

I stand up, but continue to hold Henry's hand. "Hi, Fran."

"Randy," she says, the chill in her voice well below the temperature of this air-conditioned office. "We need to get Henry home now. He has day camp to go to."

"We're making Popsicle-stick airplanes!" Henry tells me.

I smile at him. "Okay. That sounds like fun."

I let go of his hand and feel as though I'm cutting off part of my own body. I try to catch Violet's gaze, but she won't look at me. "Vi? Please think about what I said."

She exchanges a look with her mom. I have no idea what passes between them.

I get down on my knees once more. "One more hug, buddy?"

My little boy's in my arms once more. I don't want to let him go.

But I do. I have to.

Chapter Twenty-One

JOHN

I wait for Randy on a patio the coffee shop has created on the sidewalk. They've made borders with potted plants around the half dozen or so wrought-iron bistro tables and chairs. Aunt Annie's isn't a chain—it's like someone's home. Inside, there are piles of old board games, used books, and magazines like *People* and *Entertainment Weekly*. I nabbed an old issue of the latter with K.D. Lang on the cover. I love her.

But I can't read because I'm too busy keeping my eye on the shadowed area beneath the L stop at Jarvis. I've been waiting, nursing coffee with lots of cream and sugar, for a couple of hours, wanting to be there to hear the good news...or the bad. I know Randy is meeting with his soon-to-be-ex-wife at his lawyer's office downtown. He told me this morning, as we showered together in the clawfoot tub, that he thought he could talk some sense into Violet and maybe convince her that keeping the circle of people who love Henry as wide and accessible as possible is good parenting. "Vi's a good person," he said, the hope wafting off him like the aroma of the Irish Spring soap we're sharing. "If I can just talk to her, I can help her see that it's not right to keep Henry away from his dad."

His hope had been so fierce, I couldn't bring myself to tell him to lower his expectations, that people who would steal his son away from him behind his back weren't the most likely to listen to reason—from a queer. I have a sense that Violet's parents, if not Violet herself, subscribe to the mindset that being gay is a choice and, even darker, that gay men prey on little boys.

So, I want to be close when he comes back from downtown. We can celebrate with dinner at Leona's if all goes well. And, if not, I have ways to console Randy if only for long enough to give him a little island of oblivion.

I've been staying at his place in Rogers Park since the night I called him and he invited me over.

"You know what you said to me once? About me being a drowning man and you're something I'm holding onto so I can keep my head above water?" He asked me this in the wee hours of that morning when I came over, when the first thing we did was rip the clothes from each other and wrestle around on the sheets. After, we talked. I nodded when he asked me this because, indeed, I had said it. And now, I wanted to take it back.

Randy had gone on in that pillow talk, saying, "You were right. My fears and my despair, especially over my son, were pushing me beneath the waves. And, John, oh John, you seem like the only figure on shore that I can grab onto. It's true. I need you in a way that might not be comfortable for you. I need you to keep me afloat. I need you to risk being dragged in and pulled under yourself as I fight these rising tides."

Okay, so maybe he didn't put it quite so succinctly or poetically, but he did get across the point that I could be a comfort, a shoulder to cry on, support in a time of desperate need.

And, as I rode over on an empty L train, I'd known I was already ready to be those things for Randy.

Because, despite Vince's very common sense warnings and my own logical and deep misgivings, I realized how much I love this man. That's why I couldn't let him go, in both my dreams and waking life. That's why no one else held any genuine appeal for me, as cute or available as they may be.

Love isn't about being with the person who makes the most sense. It's about what's in your heart. Love doesn't show up and ask if the time is right or even if the person is right. Love just is. And I know, deep in my heart, I love Randy. And, more than anything, I want to be there for him—for better or for worse, as they say. We may never be able to get married for real in our lifetime, but we can make the promises to each other.

I lean back in my chair, my cup of coffee gone tepid despite the heat and humidity that surrounds me like a heavy blanket, too warm and too heavy. I'd ordered a scone and tried to eat it, but I was too keyed up. My gut didn't see the appeal or, as my mom used to tell me, my eyes were bigger than my stomach.

I look west, toward the train tracks that run above the street. Beyond it, the sky is the color of skim milk, but it's pretty because the clouds look like dark smudges on the gray-white surface.

The leaves in the trees hang down, not moving.

Annie herself, a big woman in a red apron and a housedress, pads out to my table. Her weight and age, both considerable, make it hard for her to move, but she smiles at me anyway. "Can I get you anything else? Refill?" She looks down at the plate with the scone and points. "You didn't like my maple scone? You're the first!" she laughs. "I'm happy to get you something else. I bake it all myself. I have some German chocolate cupcakes in there that'll rock your world."

I smile. "Thanks. Maybe later." I size her up, noticing the cropped gray hair almost a flat top, the big earrings, and the kindness in her eyes. Does she go to my church? Does it matter? She seems like the soul of kindness, so I test the waters and say, "I'm waiting for my boyfriend. Maybe when he gets here, we'll take you up on those cupcakes."

That makes her smile. "Okay, bud. That'll be if there are any left."

She walks away. I'm just about to pick up the magazine again when I hear the train rumble and screech into the station. I set the magazine down and watch as the train pulls out of the station above and the commuters begin to emerge from the station below. Because there hasn't been a train for a while, there's quite a crowd coming out, but I don't see Randy among them.

Until I do.

He's one of the last to come out. The slump of his shoulders and the way he stares down at the sidewalk tells me that things haven't gone well. His demeanor, sad from even a block away, causes my hope to plummet and a chill to rise up within me despite how hot it is.

He crosses the street quickly even though his footsteps are shuffling. There's an auto body repair place across from the station, and when they're not closed, they leave the gates to their yard and parking area open, making for a handy shortcut over Fargo and our apartment. Randy heads through it, disappearing from my view.

Did I just say *our* apartment? I smile at the slip and know that the truth will most likely become literal in the very near future.

I get up, throw some bills on the table, way more than the cost of my coffee and scone, but Annie, if that's her name, has been nice to me, understanding instinctively that I was on pins and needles, waiting.

I rush west up Jarvis and head through the auto body shop's gates myself. Randy's just ahead, about to come out on to Fargo Avenue. I push myself to run faster so I can catch up with him.

He looks over at me as I fall into step beside him. He stops. "Where did you come from?"

"That little coffee shop on Jarvis? Aunt Annie's?"

"I love that place. They have the best coffee *and* the best baked goods."

I think of my uneaten scone.

We walk on in silence. I want to give him the opportunity to talk without pressure. We both know where he's been; he'd fretted about it all last night, tossing and turning next to me. I doubt he slept at all.

The sky ahead of us is darkening and, underneath the heat, there's a crispness to the air that predicts autumn's arrival. Another train, close on the heels of the one Randy just got off, rumbles by above us. Typical CTA. No trains for a long time, then two in a row.

We turn onto Fargo and cross Ashland. I peer up at our balcony and see the herbs I planted—mint, basil, and parsley—wilting on the concrete edge. They'll perk up with a bit of water and evening's relatively cooler temperatures.

I wish I could say the same for Randy.

I get out the keys he's given me before he has a chance to wrestle his own out of his khaki's pockets. "Allow me." I unlock the outer door and wait in the vestibule as he takes the mail out of the mailbox.

"All junk." He tosses it into the wastebasket the management company has thoughtfully installed in the vestibule for just this purpose.

I unlock the second door, and Randy follows me up the stairs. We get to the front door and I open it. Once inside, I take him in my arms and hold him, not saying anything. The apartment is stuffy, hot. The thick air has rolled in through all the open windows, and it feels just as bad in here as it does outside. I can turn the fans on, but all they'll do is displace the hot air, moving it but not cooling it.

"Let's go out for dinner," I say. Earlier, I hoped a dinner out would be celebratory, but it can also be conciliatory.

Randy says nothing but moves into the bedroom. I follow him and watch as he sheds clothes he never wears in his normal life—the khakis, the plaid shirt, the loafers—to change into camo shorts and a black tank top. Part of me wants to jump his bones as he stands before me in only a pair of striped boxer shorts and the other part wants to make him a cup of tea, to draw a bath, to put some soothing music on—cue up the Kitaro.

After he's dressed, he crosses the room and turns on the box fan we have in the big window facing the street.

Over its roar, he shouts, "I don't know if I feel like going out."

"How about if I make you a cup of tea? Or no, pour you a glass of wine? Draw a nice bath for you?" I move out to the adjoining living room and slip *Silk Road* into the cassette player. Kitaro's somber, yet soothing, chords fill the air.

Randy stands behind me. "You're sweet."

I take him in my arms, hold him, kiss him. Pulling back, I touch his face, run my finger along his lips. Never breaking eye contact, I finally say, "Things didn't go well."

"Are you asking?" he wonders, sad.

"No. I'm not blind."

He tells me how the meeting went (nowhere). He plops down on the couch. "How about that wine?"

I hurry out to the kitchen and pull the cork on the bottle of red we had with our spaghetti the night before. I fill two glasses and come back. After handing him his glass and setting my own on the coffee table, I settle in beside him. "I'm sorry to hear that. Do you think things will work out better once you *do* go to court? Surely, the judge will see things more clearly and not deny you your rights."

"What *rights*? What rights, John? I'm a homosexual who left his wife to fuck other men. I'm a queer who probably shouldn't be hanging around unsupervised with little boys. That's how the judge will see things. I don't kid myself anymore." He sips his wine and chokes a bit on it.

When he looks up at me, tears stand in his eyes. "I'm gonna lose my little boy. I just know it."

I take the glass from him and, once again, hold him close. I stroke his hair and whisper, "You don't know that. There's no point in getting yourself all worked up until you know more, sweetheart."

I feel like I'm lying. And I suspect Randy knows it too.

We sit in silence, watching as shadows claim the room around us and it gets darker, darker.

At last, Randy stands up. "Yeah. Let's go out and get something to eat. Leona's?"

"Sure."

I take his hand and we head out into the night.

I don't let go of his hand once we get outside. Fuck the world if they don't approve of our love. It's just that—love.

"Can we walk to Leona's?" Randy asks. "I don't feel like getting back on the L."

"Sure." Leona's, an Italian joint on Sheridan Road, is probably only about a mile away. "Let's walk along the lakefront, okay?"

"Maybe we'll catch a breeze, if we're lucky."

We head east on Fargo, toward the band of blue-gray water at the very end of the street. We may not be able to stay next to the water the whole way to the restaurant, but I'm going to do my best to make sure that we keep the proximity as close as possible. I like the feel of Randy's hand in mine, and I feel a sense of pride that this is my man.

"We are," I say as we start down the steps leading to the beach at the street's end.

"We are what?"

"Lucky. You said we'd catch a breeze if we're lucky. And we are. Breeze or not. I'm so lucky I found you, Randy. And I like to think that, one day, you'll see you're lucky too. I hope you'll feel lucky to have found me, but even more, I hope you'll appreciate that you've found your essential self at last—the real you.

"And he's a guy worth loving."

Randy stares out at the calm water and says nothing. I hope his heart hears me.

Chapter Twenty-Two

VIOLET

Something wakes me. I sit up in my old four-poster canopy bed, feeling as though I've time traveled back to my girlhood. I rack my brain to see if I can jar loose some dream images, whatever it was that woke me and left me feeling, upon waking, a little breathless, a little sweaty despite the frigid air-conditioning in my parents' house.

All I can recall is an image of Randy at the edge of a large body of water—maybe Lake Michigan, maybe the ocean. He's poised at the top of a mass of boulders. The waves are huge, the water a dark gray.

I sit up and shiver, wrapping my arms around myself. I know it's hot outside, but is it really necessary to set the thermostat at seventy? This house feels like a mausoleum.

There's something foreboding about my dream. I don't want to follow up on that half-remembered image too closely for fear of seeing something I don't want to see.

He's in the water, drowned. The waves toss his body to and fro until he disappears beneath them.

Odd. These late-night hours here in Evanston, away from the sound of the L rumbling by outside, the traffic, and the voices on the street make it hard for me to sleep. Here, it's too quiet. The quiet has a roar of its own: lifeless, yet irritating.

Who the hell finds it too quiet to sleep?

I glance over at the bed across the room where Henry's been sleeping. His mop of dark hair, so like his dad's, isn't sticking out from under the covers. Maybe he's completely under. He does that sometimes—but only since we moved up here with Mom and Dad. I can't blame him for disappearing beneath the bed clothes since it's so damn cold in this room.

He's hiding when he does that. It's not because of the cold.

I pad silently across the plush green carpet and lean over the bed. The moonlight's enough to see by, giving everything a silvery glow. I can tell pretty quickly he's not there. There's no little shape under the floral yellow-and-green comforter. I pull back the bedclothes anyway and am rewarded with a view of empty sheets. I turn and glance toward the en suite bath, but the door yawns open, revealing a dark room.

The digital clock on my nightstand tells me it's a little after midnight.

"Henry?" I wonder out loud.

I grab my robe from the foot of the bed and shrug into it, grateful for its warmth. Once the sash is tied, I head out of the room along the narrow hallway and then make a right to descend the curving staircase.

I can barely hear my mother's voice, coming from the general vicinity of the kitchen. As I step off the bottom step, her words are just a low murmur, but there's an intensity to them that intrigues me.

I tiptoe through the living room and stand in the darkness of the dining room where I can peer into the brightly lit kitchen. At the moment, neither Mom nor Henry has seen me. I feel invisible. I pause, watching, reminded of my own childhood in that very kitchen. Mom has made Henry a glass of warm milk and, as she often does, paired it with a couple of oatmeal raisin cookies. There's a Golden book on the table, *The Poky Little Puppy*. It was mine years ago, and I'm surprised it's still around. It seems too childish, even for Henry.

Henry must have had trouble sleeping, not surprising after his encounter with his dad earlier in the day.

I smile for a moment at the scene.

But then the smile vanishes when I hear what Mom is saying.

"He doesn't love you, Henry, not really. A father who leaves his family doesn't care about his kids. You're better off without him, trust your grandma on that."

"But he *does*, Grandma. He told me today. Why can't I see him?"

Mom shakes her head and sighs. "Oh sweetheart, I hate to be the one to tell you this, but your father lies. He lied to your mom when he married her; he lied to all of us, and now he's lying to you. Don't fall for it. Your real family's right here in this house. And we know how to love you. Not like him. It's sad, but your daddy doesn't know what real love is, not really. He's a selfish man, Henry. You're better off without him."

My mouth has gone dry. I feel an ache deep in my bones as my son stares at his grandmother, eyes wide. The hurt in those eyes breaks my heart. He ignores the milk and cookies and sticks his thumb in his mouth. I haven't seen him do that in a couple of years. It gives me a nauseous feeling.

After a moment, his head drops, and he stares down at the table.

Mom pulls his thumb roughly out of his mouth. "Come on, Henry. Big boys don't suck their thumbs. It'll give you buck teeth." She shoves the glass toward him. "Drink your milk, and then we'll get you back in your bed. I'll tuck you in and read you a story."

I step into the kitchen. The bright lights hurt my eyes. "I can take care of him, Mom."

Henry looks up at me, almost confused, as though I'm a ghost or an image from a dream. "Mom?"

I smile and hope there's some comfort in that expression. "I woke up, and you weren't there." I give a little mock shiver. "I was afraid. I need my little guy to protect me. Won't you come back to bed?" I hold out my hand.

Henry slides off the chair, runs to me, and takes my hand. I squeeze it, trying to transfer my own warmth to him.

We head toward the hallway off the kitchen. At the entryway, I pause and look back at Mom. "I'll get him settled. You stay there, okay? I want to talk to you."

"Can it wait until morning, dear? I'm beat."

I almost say okay, just to avoid conflict, but then I reconsider. "No, Mom. It can't. I'll be right back down." Even though it goes against every grain in my body, I smile at her—more for Henry than for Mom.

I lead Henry back upstairs by the hand, trying to breathe normally, to walk normally to make it appear as though his mother isn't consumed by rage.

I lead him to his bed and get him tucked in, smoothing down the covers over him. I sit on the edge of the bed. "Honey, if you ever have trouble sleeping, please don't leave the room without waking me up. I promise I won't mind. And if you're havin' a bad dream? Just come over and crawl into bed with me, and I'll chase that mean old nightmare away. Okay?"

He nods. I rustle his hair and watch as he turns on his side. Ah, the sweet innocence of youth. I know he'll be asleep within minutes. He sticks his thumb back in his mouth. I'm about to reach out to stop him, to tell him the same old wives' tale about his teeth Mom just told him, but I stop myself.

I don't say or do anything.

If he needs a little comfort right now, who am I to take it away?

I plant a kiss on his cheek. "I'm gonna go back downstairs and talk to Grandma. You go back to sleep, okay? I'll be back real soon." I start out and then turn back. "And honey? Your daddy's a good man. Don't let anyone tell you otherwise."

"Okay, Mom," he mumbles over the thumb in his mouth.

"Sweet dreams," I call from the doorway. But he's already asleep.

I envy him. But as a mom, what I need to do is protect him. Show him right from wrong.

I go back downstairs.

Mom's in the kitchen, washing up the glass and plate she used with Henry even though she has a dishwasher. I stand in the entryway, waiting for her to notice me. She hums as she washes the dishes. She places them on a dish towel next to the sink to dry and wipes her hands on her quilted bathrobe.

She looks exhausted. And a little crazy, if I'm honest. There's something Stepford Wives about her and this perfect kitchen, this perfect house where not even a dust mote is allowed to survive. She can't leave even a glass unwashed, a crumb on the table.

Is she happy? Or does she simply need to be in control?

She looks up when something clues her in to me standing there, watching.

"Oh, you're back. What did you want to talk about?"

"Can we sit down?" I don't wait for an answer. It's not really a question, anyway. I pull out a chair and wait for her to join me at the table. I think about getting up and grabbing a couple of Archway cookies from the pantry, scattering crumbs on the pristine floor and tabletop, but I keep that impulse in check.

"What's up?" She sits down opposite me.

"You can't talk to him that way."

She cocks her head. "What do you mean? What way?"

"You can't say those things about Randy, his dad. You don't do me or Henry any favors when you try to turn him against a father who loves him, Mom."

"Loves him?"

"Yes. Randy adores that boy."

She blows out a disgusted sigh. "Randy apparently adores boys in general."

I hold up a hand. "Don't. It's beneath you."

She starts to say something else, but I interrupt before she can even get a single word out. "I'm not going to keep Henry from his father."

"I thought we discussed this. With your father and the lawyer. We won't lose. We'll get full custody, especially when we make it clear to the judge that his dad is a homosexual."

"We're *not* making that clear to the judge. The only person we're gonna make it clear to is Henry, in terms a child can understand. And we're gonna do that so Henry can grow up knowing there are different kinds of folks in the world, and all of them—all of them, Mother—are worthy of love." I shake my head. I want to scream at her. Call her a bigot. But I know if I'm to get through, even the tiniest bit, I have to stay calm.

"Henry needs to see his dad. On a regular basis. I won't try to keep him from Randy. I can't. I want my boy to have all the love that's available to him. Love's a rare commodity in this world, don't you think?"

I pause. Mom crosses her arms and stares off into the distance.

I get up. "If the condo and you guys paying for my lawyer is conditional on me dancing to your tune, then forget it. I'll find a way to take care of us, and I'll find a way to not turn this into a battle for something I don't even believe in. If you agree with me, though, and can see that Henry needs his daddy, then we can continue to work together to look for compromises and solutions. But I won't be the person Henry grows up hating because I kept him away from a perfectly decent and loving father. I don't think you want him to grow up hating you guys either.

"Because, trust me, you won't win. Even if we got no visitation, or supervised strictly, it's a loss. For our boy. And your efforts to turn your grandson against his father will only make him resent you, maybe even hate you.

"I know this much is true."

I said it. I said everything I wanted to say.

"We'll have to discuss this with your father, of course."

"Of course. But it won't change anything, not on this point anyway."

Since there's nothing more to say without belaboring the point, I get up from the table. I feel as though a weight has been lifted from my shoulders. I don't allow doubt or worry to creep in.

Mom calls out as I enter the dark hallway leading to the stairs. "I'll go to the church in the morning and light a candle for you."

I start up the stairs. "You do that, Mom. I need *all* the help I can get."

1986, Autumn

Sonnet 73
That time of year thou mayst in me behold
When yellow leaves, or none, or few, do hang
Upon those boughs which shake against the cold,
Bare ruin'd choirs where late the sweet birds sang.
In me thou seest the twilight of such day
As after sunset fadeth in the west,
Which by and by black night doth take away,
Death's second self, that seals up all in rest.
In me thou see'st the glowing of such fire
That on the ashes of his youth doth lie,
As the death-bed whereon it must expire,
Consum'd with that which it was nourished by.
This thou perceiv'st, which makes thy love more strong,
To love that well which thou must leave ere long.
—William Shakespeare

Chapter Twenty-Three

RANDY

Fall is just about over, at least that's what the calendar says. But that calendar? Big liar, always has been.

Winter "officially" arrives next week.

The weather outside our front windows, though, tells a different story. That view says fall has been over for a while, claimed by the brutal Chicago winter. Snow comes down hard outside, blanketing the grimy city streets with a layer of pristine white. It's beautiful...and deceptively inviting.

It's Saturday morning. John's in the kitchen, making bacon and eggs and coffee. The smells and the coziness of being inside are a comfort. This little apartment is a sanctuary, a buffer against the cold and the damp. John hums something tuneless, yet cheery, in the kitchen as he fries our bacon and scrambles our eggs.

So much has changed in the past couple of months that, when I think about all the upheaval and shifting, I almost get a little dizzy. I sometimes have to look again just to recognize my own life.

Looking around from my perch here on the couch, I have to admit that, if anyone else saw this mess, they'd think both John and I are crazy. Hoarders. For one, there are boxes everywhere—in the kitchen, in the dining room, both bedrooms. Some of them are open with clothes, books, spatulas, sporting equipment, and whatever accouterments make up a life, spilling out. Some are still taped shut.

John just moved in with me officially at the beginning of December, when he could get out of his own lease, although we've been spending just about every night together for months now.

It feels like he just came into my life yesterday.

It feels like he's been with me forever.

I wake in the morning sometimes and watch him as he sleeps, the curly dark hair against the white pillowcase, the easy rise and fall of that broad chest. Even when he snores, I find it a comfort rather than an annoyance. There's something oddly soothing about the buzz saw noises he makes.

We've settled into an easy routine side-by-side. I can't wait to get home from work to see him. And when he's gone at the fire station, my heart aches with longing as though a piece of me is missing.

But his unpacked boxes and piles of clothes on the floor of the master bedroom walk-in closet aren't the only clutter in our little world.

No. Christmas is right around the corner.

And Henry adores Christmas. The carols. The decorations. The TV specials (Charlie Brown!). But most of all, Santa Claus.

We've set up a tree in almost every room. In the living room, there's the big real one, purchased from a lot over on Sheridan. A traditional Douglas fir, we've decked it out in white lights, candy canes, and red velvet ribbons. Crowded underneath are dozens of presents—for me, for John, most especially for Henry (although we hold some back because of Santa Claus), and even a sweater and necklace for Violet.

The dining room has one of those retro silver metallic trees, artificial to the max. Decorated only with red balls, it changes color because of a rotating tri-colored projecting light at its base. Henry's fascinated by it.

The kitchen and other rooms all have small artificial trees that we picked up at K-Mart. These all have their own twinkling multicolored lights and sit in little burlap bag bases.

We do this for Henry, who will be coming over for his Saturday visit in a couple of hours.

I close my eyes, so grateful that Violet stood up for him and for herself and didn't allow her parents to attempt to hijack my son's love away from me. I feel like I narrowly averted death. And life without my boy? I shake my head. Even with John's love and the warmth of him beside me, I don't think I could manage to have much of a life if Henry was kept away from me.

I don't know what caused Violet to stick up for me and my rights as a dad. We haven't ever really talked much about it, partly because I don't like to, as the saying goes, look a gift horse in the mouth.

I want to believe, simply, that Violet saw it was the right thing to do. Keeping a boy from a father who loves him would have just been cruel. And yet, I had a real fear that would be just what would happen. I had nightmares about it. Anxiety attacks.

But love won. Love always wins.

I know Violet paid dearly for sticking up for my rights as a father. Her parents helping her out with a new home and paying for her lawyer were both swept from the table when she refused to petition for sole custody.

With their so-called *help*, things would have been ugly and financially draining. No one would have come out of things better off if we'd followed Violet's parents' footsteps into hate and discrimination.

In the end, though, I like to believe she's happier. More her own person. She and Henry have a small apartment in Wilmette, less than a half hour north. She's training for her stockbroker license and expects to move up in the company she works for next year.

Henry comes over on Wednesdays for dinner. John and I usually pick out a good video from the store down on Clark Street and order pizza from Giordano's.

He's here every Saturday, too, back in his old bedroom (the only room in the little apartment uncluttered by John's boxes) for the night. I have yet to take for granted getting him into his pj's, having him brush his teeth, and reading him yet another chapter from *The Wizard of Oz* books that I adored as a boy. I see all the characters and fantastic situations in those books anew through Henry's eyes.

And I shudder to think how close I came to losing him.

Violet and I used a mediator, and we sat down and talked, much more productively than our first sit-down at my lawyer's, and worked things out. Like adults. Like co-parents. Like friends.

We're still working on that last part, but things get better all the time. And Violet loves John! Sometimes, I think she prefers his company to my own. I tell myself that's only because he doesn't come with any of the baggage that still sits between us, even though that pile of luggage gets smaller and smaller as more and more time passes.

Violet has been going to PFLAG meetings. She's trying to understand, trying to be supportive. The man in her life fell away when she told him her husband was gay. I think, although he didn't say, he was afraid of AIDS.

Who *isn't* afraid of AIDS these days?

I'm so glad I found John, and it's just the two of us in our bed. He's told me about his friend Dean...

"Breakfast is ready, sir!" John calls from the kitchen.

I smile and get up to join him.

I pad barefoot into the dining room. The sunlight pours in through the three windows on the northern wall, the golden illumination boosted by the snow covering the ground outside. Our windows are level with the tracks, and a train sits outside, waiting to go into the terminus of the line at Howard Street.

I can see people on the train, peering in our windows.

"You should shut those blinds," John says as he spies the people spying on us.

"Why? Let them look." I come up behind him and wrap my arms around him. I glance out the window and then plant a kiss on his neck.

He nearly drops the plate he's holding. "You know that drives me insane."

He turns and kisses me and then says, a little breathlessly, "I went to all this trouble. Let's take a few minutes to enjoy it. I mean—bacon. Then—*bed*."

Reluctantly, I sit at the table and smile across at him, thinking how this little domestic moment is the answer to all my dreams.

I CLOSE *THE Wizard of Oz* and smile down at Henry. He's tucked in tightly, as he likes it, and he regards me with his big hazel eyes. I've read the last two chapters of the book to him, and he seems happy, contented. But not enough, just yet, to toddle off to dreamland.

"It's different," he says.

"How so?" I ask, even though I know the answer. But I want to see how Henry puts things.

"In the movie, Dorothy realizes her whole trip to Oz was just a dream."

I nod.

"But in the book, everything really happened."

"Which way do you like better?"

"I like both of them, but if I have to pick..." Henry's voice trails off sleepily as he thinks about it. His thumb wanders up to his mouth, seemingly of its own accord. Even though I don't stop him, he pulls it away just before it goes in his mouth. "I'd pick the book. Because I like that it's all real. If it was just a dream, she would have never met the Cowardly Lion, or the Tin Man, or even the Scarecrow." He ponders things for a bit more and then says, "Plus I like that she left home and then found her way back. If it was just a dream, she never left home in the first place."

"And why does that matter?"

"Because sometimes you need to leave home to appreciate it, to know where you belong."

What he says brings a lump to my throat. I know he's talking about his time at his grandparents. Time I feel guilty for having put him through. And I'm reminded to be grateful that he's here—home—now.

I lean down and kiss him. "Even though Mommy and Daddy live in different places, you always have a home, Henry, you know that."

"I know." I can tell by the way his head sinks more into the pillow that he's about to surrender over to sleep. It's been a long battle tonight, what with Dorothy and her pals keeping him excited, but the time has come. I tuck the covers in even more tightly and stand.

I move to the door, and he asks me to leave the hall light on.

"Pancakes in the morning?"

"Please...and thank you."

I close the door, feeling a rush of gratitude for having my son with me under the same roof.

Home.

IN THE BEDROOM, John's already asleep. I should be disappointed, but the fact that he's there is enough.

I undress in the dark, thinking how I'll pick up my clothes from the floor when morning's light creeps in through the partially open blinds.

Naked, I shiver and hurry to get under the covers.

The bed is warm. John's like a furnace, and his body heat has made the comforter and the flannel sheet toasty. I sink down into heaven.

And John turns to me, sleepy, and plants a kiss sloppily on my eyebrow. His body is even warmer, and I melt into it.

Home.

Present Day, Winter

"When you do things from your soul, you feel a river moving in you, a joy."
—Rumi

Epilogue

RANDY

A little breathless, I reach the top of the rise called Notch Number Four on the trail. The vista before me—the pines, the blue-gray mountain peaks, the dun color of the Coachella Valley spread out before us in all its desert glory—is breathtaking.

The contrast is remarkable. Here we all are, nearly 9,000 feet up, almost at the top of Mount San Jacinto. The air is crisp, clean, and cold enough to require winter coats, boots, gloves, scarves, and woolen caps. It's probably only in the twenties up here.

Less than an hour ago, we were turning off Palm Canyon to wend our way up the road leading to the Palm Springs Aerial Tramway. It was sunny and seventy-five degrees. The sun was so intense it felt even warmer.

And now, after a ten-minute, swaying tram ride up the side of a craggy mountain, we are deep into winter. Snow blankets the ground all around us, tamped down in places on the trail to become ice. We have to watch our steps.

They've all come out to visit John and me in Palm Springs for the Yuletide holidays. John and I moved here a few years ago when John retired from the fire department, and I got my first book contract for what John calls, "yet another Dystopian thriller." We have a little condo with its own pool in our private backyard and love the slow ease of the desert as compared to Chicago and its crime and ridiculous pace, not to mention the horrors of winter by Lake Michigan.

This is the first time all of us have been together in years.

I allow myself to sit on a big rock even though it freezes my ass. I lean back now and observe what I've always dreamed of having and at times wasn't sure I ever would—*my family*.

Looking out at the picture-postcard view from the top of the rise are Violet and her husband, Keith, a fellow stockbroker. The two of them now own an apartment building in the Edgewater neighborhood of Chicago, taking the top floor—and its awesome city and lake views—for themselves. They've been together almost as long as John and I have. Three decades. They're happy too. And it warms me to know that Violet, despite the rocky road we traveled together, eventually found her own happily ever after. It's a bonus that Keith is a man I like, admire, and respect. Open-minded and compassionate, he's a great husband to Vi and a great stepfather to Henry.

I couldn't have asked for better.

Violet turns abruptly and looks up at me. She holds a hand at the level of her forehead to block the intense sun, grins, and begins making her way up to where I stand.

Next to me, she links our arms. "It's beautiful up here. Thanks for thinking of this."

"Isn't it gorgeous? It almost doesn't seem real."

Together, we stare out at alpine wilderness, jaw-dropping expanses, and an endless blue sky, dotted with a few clouds that make me think, oddly, of flying saucers.

After a time, I say, quietly, "Thank you."

I turn to her and look into her pale-blue eyes. I take in how much older she is—the crow's feet around her eyes, the laugh lines framing her mouth, how her blonde hair is gray at the roots and not as lustrous as it once was. She's thicker around the middle. But then, who among us isn't? But even with all this, I still see the young woman I married. A sudden vision comes to me.

We were only married a couple of weeks and taking the subway downtown to get to our respective jobs. It was summer and Violet wore a white gauzy dress, with tiny blue polka dots, belted at the waist. Her blonde hair was cut in a shoulder-length bob. The train was crowded. I noticed how other people, men especially, regarded her. She was lovely, young, innocent. Her hair was a silken gold. I could imagine her tentative smile. In that moment, I'd felt such tenderness for her, such love, even though there was something dark in my psyche, pulling me back, telling me that something was slightly off.

Okay, maybe more than slightly.

The fact remained back then and even now, Violet and I shared a special bond.

"For what?"

"For coming out to Palm Springs so we could have a real family holiday. For being supportive. For being you. But most of all, for sticking up for me all those years ago. For being brave enough to stand for what you knew was right. Not everyone can do that. And you did—selflessly.

"I probably wouldn't have all those special moments I did with Henry as he grew up if it wasn't for you and your love and understanding, so thank you." I swallow back the lump in my throat and laugh as I brush a couple of tears away. "I'm getting sentimental in my old age."

Violet says nothing, but she positions herself in front of me and takes me in her arms. She gives me a good squeeze. "I love you."

"And I love you," I tell her. I laugh. "Finding out I was gay was like putting down the shield and the sword, like removing the mask. It was right. But the fact is I've always also loved the company of women, their nurturing ways *and* their bitchiness." I chuckle again. "And you most of all."

She breaks away and eyes me. It looks as though she's about to say something, but all she does is take my hand and squeezes it for a moment. I watch as she returns to her husband. He smiles when she's at his side again, puts his arm around her, and points to something in the distance.

John, who's brought up the rear on the trail, just now catches up. I suppose he'd seen Violet and me together. He knows, far too well, all about the wounds from that terrible time so many years ago, when I was afraid I'd lose everything I held most dear. Old scars.

"Everything okay?" John asks.

And now it's me putting my arm around John. I squeeze him next to me, almost like I'm trying to make the two of us one. A tall order, because John, always beefy, is now more so. Some might say fat. But I call him my big lovable bear. His hair is still thick, but it's gone silver, the curls cropped short. He wears a full beard that's almost white. The lack of color in his hair just makes his eyes shine more brightly.

He's adorable. He still turns heads when we venture out to the gay bars along Arenas in downtown Palm Springs.

"Everything is fine. Couldn't be better." I plant a kiss on his cheek. "In fact, this, right here, might be one of the happiest moments of my life."

Wisely, he says nothing. He simply lays his head on my shoulder.

I bask in his comforting closeness and the rays of the sun.

"Look at those two," I say after a while.

We both peer down at Henry, now in his thirties, with his own husband, Phillipe. The two now live much too far away, in Montreal, but it makes my heart sing when I see them together because they're so suited for each other. Their happiness radiates out of them like the sun above us. They've been legally married for almost a decade now and still are the most perfect couple I know.

Henry's helping Phillipe, who's tall and gangly with a mop of perfectly straight blond hair, down onto a boulder below us. It looks treacherous, but the views have to be even more stunning the closer one gets to the edge.

I watch them settle in on the boulder, their four legs dangling.

I'm grateful that Henry's coming from a broken household hasn't affected his ability to be a good and faithful husband, to make a good marriage. I've always tried to instill in him that love is the only thing that matters and that love is never in short supply—it will always replenish itself, as long as we nurture it.

"They're so cute," John says. "We should urge them to go out for New Year's Eve. Us old folks can stay in and watch Anderson Cooper and the ball drop at nine o'clock and then go to bed."

"You make it sound so dirty," I say.

"I wish."

We both laugh, leaning even closer and leaning into our shared history. The right history—the one that's perfect for us. The one that makes us a family.

About the Author

Real Men. True Love.

Rick R. Reed draws inspiration from the lives of gay men to craft stories that quicken the heartbeat, engage emotions, and keep the pages turning. Although he dabbles in horror, dark suspense, and comedy, his attention always returns to the power of love. He's the award-winning and bestselling author of more than fifty works of published fiction and is forever at work on yet another book. Lambda Literary has called him: "A writer that doesn't disappoint..." You can find him at www.rickrreed.com or www.rickrreedreality.blogspot.com. Rick lives in Palm Springs, CA with his beloved husband and their fierce Chihuahua/Shiba Inu mix.

Email: rickrreedbooks@gmail.com

Facebook: www.facebook.com/rickrreedbooks

Twitter: @rickrreed

Coming Soon from Rick R. Reed

Sky Full of Mysteries

What if your first love was abducted and presumed dead—but returned twenty years later?

That's the dilemma Cole Weston faces. Now happily married to Tommy D'Amico, he's suddenly thrown into a surreal world when his first love, Rory Schneidmiller, unexpectedly reappears.

Where has Rory been all this time? Has he time traveled? What happened to him two decades ago, when a strange mass appeared in the night sky and lifted him into outer space? Rory has no memory of those years. For him, it's as though only a day or two has passed.

Rory still loves Cole with the passion unique to young first love. Cole has never forgotten Rory, yet Tommy has been his rock, by his side since Rory disappeared.

Cole is forced to choose between an idealized and passionate first love and the comfort of a long-term marriage. How can he decide? Who faces this kind of quandary, anyway? The answers might lie among the stars...

Also Available from NineStar Press

Connect with NineStar Press

www.ninestarpress.com

www.facebook.com/ninestarpress

www.facebook.com/groups/NineStarNiche

www.twitter.com/ninestarpress

www.tumblr.com/blog/ninestarpress